RYAN REDEMPTION

SADIE KINCAID

RED HOUSE PRESS

NEW YORK RUTHLESS

Ryan Redemption is a Dark Mafia, reverse harem romance that deals with mature themes which may be triggering for some.

It is Book 2 in the New York Ruthless Series, featuring the Jessie and The Ryan Brothers and follows on directly from Book 1 which should be read first.

Click here to read Ryan Rule or visit Amazon.com

CHAPTER 1

JESSIE

*M*y eyes fly open and I turn beneath the covers as someone knocks loudly at the door. Blood thunders in my ears and I blink in the faint light of the room, as for a few, heart-stopping moments, I don't recognize any of my surroundings.

"Jessica. Your father wishes for you to join him for breakfast," a voice calls through the closed door. A wave of relief washes over me as the deep, Russian accent reminds me I am in my father's house. The voice belongs to Vlad, the bear-like man I first met outside the Ryan brothers' apartment building in New York three days ago. I have since learned he is my father's most trusted soldier, and I have spoken more with Vlad these past three days than I have with my papa.

"I'll be there soon," I shout and the sound of my own voice, and the effort of speaking, makes my head hurt. I screw my eyes closed as pain tightens like a band around my forehead. My throat is dry and sore and I reach for the glass of water on my nightstand. A book clatters to the floor and I remember I was reading in bed last night, but I must have dozed off mid-chapter.

That's so unlike me. Ordinarily, I struggle to switch my brain off to fall asleep so easily. I take a sip of the water and it soothes my raw throat. I'm sure I'm coming down with a cold.

As I pick up the book, I glance at the front cover and a sudden rush of sadness almost overwhelms me as I recall how Conor used to read to me, and how the velvety growl of his voice always made me feel so safe and content. Surely it wasn't all a lie?

It's been three days since I walked out of the penthouse apartment in New York, leaving only a note for the brothers. The four men who I thought were my new family. The men I had fallen completely in love with, and who I believed loved me too. That was all until I met a ghost who turned my world upside down and who told me that everything I believed to be true was a lie. The shock of seeing him standing there in front of me made me lose all sense of logic and reason.

I watched my father die ten years ago. He was slaughtered by an assassin who killed my entire family and then kidnapped me before keeping me prisoner for almost two years. Except that now I'm forced to believe that my papa didn't die at all. Somehow, he survived that attack and he has been looking for me ever since.

Tears spring to my eyes as I run my hand over the smooth book cover, tracing my fingertips over the gold embossed letters of Leo Tolstoy's name. A few days ago, I was the happiest I had been in my adult life. Seeing my father again and learning that he is alive should make me happy too. But I can't stop thinking about everything that I've left behind. I have so many questions that when I have the opportunity to ask one, I become tongue-tied and don't know where to start. This isn't helped by the fact that whilst my father promised me he would answer all my queries, I have barely seen him since we arrived at this house.

My memory of my drive to this place is something of a daze. I remember holding my father's hand. We drank some zavarka -

Russian tea - and the next thing I knew we were here and my father had to rush off to attend to some urgent business. Vlad has since told me he's had lots of pressing matters to attend to recently, and from everything I have witnessed here so far, my father works for the Bratva, and is very close to the top. I hope he is still searching for the Wolf as well as me. Surely he must be?

I jump out of bed and walk to the bathroom. If my father wants me to have breakfast with him, perhaps I will finally get some answers.

ONCE I'VE SHOWERED and dressed, I make my way downstairs and into the large dining room to find my father already seated and waiting for me.

"Good morning, printsessa. Come. Eat with me," he says with a smile as he gestures to the place setting opposite him.

"Morning, Papa," I say as I slide into the seat.

He reaches out and cups my chin with his palm. "You look tired. Are you feeling well?" he frowns.

"I think I'm coming down with something."

"I'll have Marfa make you some more of her soup," he says with a nod. "You'll be feeling better in no time."

"Thank you, Papa," I smile. Marfa is a wonderful cook and she has been feeding me up since I got here.

As though he has conjured her up with the mere mention of her name, Marfa walks into the room carrying a tray of zavarka, ponchiki and pancakes and sets them down before us with a polite nod of her head. I have hardly heard her speak more than two words since my arrival, despite my trying to engage her in conversation on many occasions. After she leaves the room, my father piles his plate high, and I smile as I watch him eat. He never used to have such a sweet tooth. I much prefer coffee and cereal for breakfast myself, but Marfa makes delicious traditional

Russian food, and I take some pancakes and put them onto my plate.

While my father continues enjoying his breakfast, I pick up my fork, but my hand hovers over my food. "Can we talk about what happened, Papa?" I ask, and he frowns deeply.

"Jessica! We are eating!"

"I realize that. But I need to know what happened. You said we could talk."

He places his silverware down onto the table and stares at me, and I swallow under his intense gaze. When I arrived here a few days earlier, I waited up for him after he was called away on business, but I fell asleep in the large armchair by a roaring fire in the sitting room. The following morning he had left again before I was awake. The only other times I have seen him, he has been in a hurry or we have been eating and he has admonished me for spoiling his appetite.

"What do you want to know?" he asks with a deep sigh.

"That night at our house. How did you get out of there?"

"I told you, it was a miracle. I woke up in a hospital bed. You were gone and your mother and brothers were dead."

"Do you know why it happened? Why the Wolf came for us?"

"Your mother and I left Russia because we were running from the Bratva."

"The mob?"

"Yes."

"Why were you running?"

He closes his eyes for a moment and runs a hand over his beard. "That is too long a story for this morning, printsessa. Perhaps some other time."

"But, Papa..."

"Jessica!" he interrupts me. "Can we not just enjoy our breakfast? I have been searching for you for ten long years. We have the rest of our lives to discuss this yurodstvo!"

Craziness! Really? I bite back the disappointment that surges through my chest, remembering how much time this man had for me when I was a child and how he loved to answer the many questions I used to constantly ask him. But, I suppose watching your wife and children being slaughtered and searching for your daughter for ten years changes a man.

"Can I ask one more question, Papa?"

He narrows his eyes at me. "Go on."

"Have you ever come close to finding the Wolf?"

The vein pulses in his temple as he clenches his jaw shut. "No," he snarls. "But now I have you to help me. You are the only person who has ever seen his face, printsessa. Together, we will find him."

Finally, something we can agree on. "We will, Papa."

That seems to please him too and he reaches for my hand. "Now that you are back by my side where you belong, there is nothing we can't do," he smiles.

"You work for the Bratva now, Papa?" I ask as I cut into my pancake.

He laughs softly. "You could say that," he nods as he pops a ponchiki into his mouth.

"Is that how you found me?"

"I thought we agreed only one more question, printsessa?" he snaps.

"I'm just making conversation," I smile.

He shakes his head softly in exasperation, but he answers me. "No. I found you because the Ryan brothers were trying to make contact with the Wolf so they could hand you back to him."

My breath catches in my throat at the mention of their name and another wave of sadness washes over me. I open my mouth to ask more questions, but my father shoots me a look that makes me close it again. My head is throbbing and I am so tired despite having slept for almost ten hours. I have far too many questions and I still know little more about anything than I did when I arrived here.

"They told you only what you wanted to hear, printsessa," he says as he places his large rough hand over mine. "Don't feel bad about being taken in by them. They are professionals."

I nod my agreement. Because the man who raised me, the one who taught me all I know, he would never lie to me.

CHAPTER 2

CONOR

*C*limbing out of the SUV, I flex my neck and listen to the satisfying crack before walking around the side of the car to join my brother, Shane. I can feel anger coming from him like heat from an inferno. It has only grown fiercer in the three days since we watched the security footage of Jessie walking out of our apartment holding some fucker's hand. Three days since she tore out our fucking hearts. I'm holding onto the hope that she didn't just choose to fuck us over like that. Maybe she was being threatened? Or blackmailed? But Shane is convinced that she has been playing us all along. He is also sure that she is working for the Bratva, and always has been.

The thought that she might be in league with the people responsible for kidnapping and torturing me two years ago makes me want to gouge out my own eyes. I will tear this city apart to find her. But I refuse to accept that the woman who shared our home, our beds and our lives, could be so cruel.

My twin brothers, Liam and Mikey, are working their way through every piece of security footage in the New York area trying to identify the car Jessie must have got into, while Shane and I are taking an entirely different approach.

"You ready?" he says as he hands me a small black holdall that contains some of my favorite toys.

"Always."

"Let's find us some fucking Russians then," he snarls, walking toward the apartment building and holding the door open for me. We take the stairs to the top floor, and along the hallway to apartment 42. It's the home of Igor Nikitin, the only surviving member of Dmitry's crew, and therefore, he is the only remaining link we have to the guy from Balthazar's bar who thought he recognized Jessie and called her Nataliya.

We reach the apartment door and I look at Shane, wondering if we're going to knock. But he lifts his right leg and brings his steel toe-capped, size-ten boot crashing against the lock, causing the door to burst open.

"Way to make an entrance, bro," I grin at him as we step into the hallway just in time to see Igor flying out of what I assume is the bathroom, with his pants around his ankles and his dick flailing in the air as he makes a run for the window. Shane reaches into my jacket pocket and takes out the screwdriver he knows I have in there before throwing it at Igor with a perfect aim. It strikes him on the back of the head, causing him to stumble against the wall and fall onto the floor with his ass in the air.

Walking further into the hallway, we haul him up and push him into the kitchen where Shane sits him down on a chair while I place my bag onto the counter and begin taking out some of the contents and placing them down.

Igor shouts in Russian and Shane punches him in the mouth, knocking out one of his teeth in the process and it clatters onto the tiled floor.

"If you don't stop fucking screaming like a pussy, I will cut out your fucking tongue," Shane snarls as he holds out his hand to me and I pass him a roll of duct tape. Our victim sees the tape and tries to jump up from the chair, earning him a swift kick in the nuts from Shane that brings tears to the Russian's eyes and makes him gasp for breath while he tries to handle the pain.

Shane works quickly, strapping him to the chair, although Igor doesn't make it easy for him. He struggles and lashes out while cursing in Russian. I could help out, but my older brother is more than capable of handling this guy alone, and besides, I enjoy watching him work. My turn will come soon enough.

Once Igor is securely bound, Shane pulls up a chair and sits directly in front of him. "I need information," he barks. "Tell me what I need to know and we might let you walk out of here."

"Fuck you!" Igor snarls, and then he spits a huge globule of saliva mixed with blood onto Shane's face and I can't help but smile. This is going to be fun.

Shane stands and takes a towel from the kitchen counter. He wipes his face before turning back to Igor, who is now eyeing him with a mixture of terror and anger in his eyes. Shane moves swiftly. Extending his hand, he takes hold of the tip of Igor's ear, and then he tears it clean off his head. It's a particular skill my older brother has that I've always been envious of.

The sudden and brutal loss of his ear causes Igor to open his mouth to howl in pain. But before the sound can come out, Shane stuffs the towel into his open mouth, muffling the noise and making Igor gag at the sudden intrusion.

As he tosses the now useless appendage onto the floor, Shane sits down again. "Shall we try this one more time?" he scowls at our captive, who nods his agreement as tears run down his face and blood from the gaping hole that was once his ear trickles down his neck, staining the collar of his pale blue shirt.

"The man who had his throat cut at Balthazar's six weeks back. The one who survived and died in hospital. Did you know his name?"

Igor nods and Shane takes the towel from his mouth.

"Viktor," he croaks.

"Who did Viktor work for?"

"For Dmitry."

"Who else?"

"No-one else," Igor shakes his head.

"He recognized a friend of ours. Her name is Jessica, but he called her Nataliya. Do either of those names mean anything to you?"

"No."

"Somebody visited Viktor in the hospital ten minutes before he died. Any idea who that was?"

"No." His head moves vigorously from side to side as though his effort might convince us that he is telling the truth.

Shane runs his hand through his hair and lets out a long, deep sigh. "We don't have fucking time for this," he says as he stands up and turns to me. "You're up."

"About time," I say as I turn to the counter and pick up the cordless drill and hammer. I have plenty more tools in my black bag of tricks, but these are two of my favorites and they're pretty effective when time is of the essence.

I move the chair out of the way and stand in front of Igor, who stares up at me, his eyes flickering between the weapons in each of my hands. "I don't know anything," he spits out as he shakes his head from side to side.

"Well, maybe you do and you just don't realize it yet," I say with a wink as I press the button on the drill and it whirs to life. The sound of trickling liquid onto the floor makes me glance down and I smile as I watch Igor pissing himself in fear.

ONE HOUR LATER, Igor lies on the floor of his kitchen with blood pouring from almost every part of his body. I was surprised by just how much pain he could take, but, I suppose when you're covering for the head of the Bratva, you keep your mouth shut as long as you can. He is close to the end, but he clings on to life in desperation, because it's human nature to fight death even when it stares us in the face.

I crouch down on my heels and lift his head by his hair, which is matted with blood. "Thank you for the information, Igor. We'll make sure that Alexei learns exactly who betrayed him." I smile at him as I watch the last spark of life flicker from behind his eyes before I stand up. Walking to the basin, I begin to wash some of his blood from my hands.

"I'll call someone in to clean this up," Shane says as he leans against the doorframe. "I wasn't sure he had anything to tell us. You have a gift, Con."

I shrug. "People always know more than they think they do."

"Hmm. I'll call the twins and tell them to meet us back at the apartment. With Igor's information we should be able to find her soon."

"That's if Jessie is linked to Alexei Ivanov, and it isn't just a coincidence that Viktor worked for him back in Russia."

"We have no other leads to go on," Shane shrugs as I dry my hands on some paper towels. "Besides, I feel like this makes sense. It all adds up. And if Jessie's family were linked to the head of the Bratva, then it would explain their murder too. The Wolf was the Bratva's top assassin."

Despite what I just said, I nod in agreement. I expect he's right too. But why the hell did Jessie walk out of our apartment, either with, or to go to, Alexei Ivanov? It doesn't make sense to me. I can only think of three plausible explanations. The one that kills me to consider is that she has been plotting against us all along, but, I hold on to the hope that there is every chance that she is that she's being played herself, or she left because she was scared of something, or someone. Although, I have to agree with Shane; she didn't appear scared when she walked into the elevator holding that guy's hand.

It still makes me sick when I recall that image of her leaving us, or when I think about the words on that note which were written as though we were nothing to her, even after we'd made it clear that she was everything to us. I can't bring myself to accept that everything we did and said was a lie. But perhaps I'm just fooling myself. I don't trust my own judgment anymore, especially when it comes to Jessica Romanov, or whoever the hell she really is.

Jessie's leaving has hit us all hard. Perhaps Shane has taken it the hardest, although he would never admit it, but it took a lot for him to let Jessie in. I've never seen him open up like that with anyone for a very long time. Her betrayal has cut him deep and I dread to think what he has in store for her when we find her. Because he is sure that she has stabbed us all in the back and right now he won't even consider an alternative explanation for her leaving.

CHAPTER 3

JESSIE

The aroma of Marfa's delicious cooking wafts along the hallway, making my stomach growl and rousing me from my sleep. I glance at the clock and realize I've slept the afternoon away. Sitting up, I shake my head to clear it and rub my temples, sure now that I am definitely coming down with the flu. I wander down the stairs and along the hallway, past the kitchen toward my father's office, my bare feet padding quietly on the wooden floor.

His door is closed, and I knock and wait to be permitted inside.

"Vkhodit!" he calls, signaling me to enter.

Opening the door, I walk inside to see him sitting at his desk with his head bent over his computer. He glances up and I smile at him. "Evening, Papa."

"Jessica," he nods. "Dinner will be served shortly."

"Great. It smells delicious," I reply as I take a seat opposite him.

He frowns at me as though my entering his office is an intrusion and an annoyance, but I'm not leaving here until I have some answers from him. He doesn't get to rip me from my new life in

New York and then refuse to speak to me about the things that are so important to me — to both of us. I had imagined that when we got to this house, we would talk long into the night and again the next day, catching up on all we had missed in the ten years since we had last seen each other, but, he had to attend to more important matters yesterday after breakfast and I haven't seen him since. "I'll see you at dinner, printsessa. I have some work to finish," he snaps.

"I need to talk to you, Papa."

"Not now," he says with a sigh, and anger begins to bubble beneath my skin.

"Then when, Papa? I have been here for four whole days and you have barely spoken to me. We have so much to talk about. So much to tell each other. Don't we? I have questions that I need answers to," I say, aware that my voice is raised, but I will not be dismissed like a child any longer.

He narrows his eyes at me and runs a hand across his thick beard. "Maybe I don't want to talk about it, Jessica!" he snaps. "I searched for you for so very long and now I have found you. That is all that matters."

"Not to me, Papa." I glare at him.

He glares back at me, his blue eyes darker than I remember. "Fine. I have five minutes," he snaps.

"Do you know anyone named Nataliya?" I ask, recalling the man who called me by that name when I was in a club with the brothers.

His jaw clenches at the sound of her name before he quickly regains his composure. "It was your mother's name. Before she left Russia."

"It was? So that was why he recognized me." I frown into the distance as I gather my thoughts. "A man called me by that name. He must have known her, Papa. Perhaps it can help us find the Wolf?"

"What man?" he snarls.

14

I lean back against my chair. "I don't know his name. And he's dead now. But he worked for Dmitry Nureyev."

"Dmitry knew nothing about the Wolf. You stay away from men like him."

"But one of his men recognized me. Or he recognized Mama. He called me Nataliya."

"Lots of people knew your Mama when we lived in Russia, printsessa. She was…" He shakes his head.

"She was what?"

For the first time since I saw him in New York, I see a flicker of emotion in his eyes. "She came from a very prominent family. She was the most beautiful woman in Moscow. She was highly prized amongst many."

"Why did you both come to America?"

He looks behind me into the distance. "We were running from some people who wanted to kill us. Your Mama did a terrible thing."

I blink at him. My mom was the most gentle and kindest woman I have ever known. What could she have possibly done that would have made them run so far and for so long? "What did she do?" I whisper.

His eyes dart back to me. "You look so much like her, printsessa. One day soon, you will marry into a good Russian family and make me lots of grand-babies," he says with a smile that doesn't quite reach his eyes.

"I don't want to get married or have babies, Papa."

He laughs softly. "Do not be ridiculous. I already have your husband in mind," he says as he stands from his chair.

"What?" I frown at him as he reaches out his hand to me.

"He's from a good family." He looks down at his outstretched hand as if to emphasize that I haven't taken it. "And don't worry, I won't tell him that you have been with any of those Irish pigs."

The anger that has been bubbling beneath my skin for the past five minutes suddenly erupts out of my chest. "I did not endure two years being the plaything of the Wolf for you to marry me off to some man I've never even met," I shout.

"Jessica!" he hisses, and something about the way he looks at me makes the blood freeze in my veins. "You will do as you are told."

I am about to reply that I won't when Marfa walks into the room. "Dinner is ready, Sir," she says quietly.

"I have business to attend to. Jessica will be eating alone," he snarls and then he strides out of his office, leaving me watching after him in a daze.

I SIT at the dining table eating the delicious soup Marfa has prepared. Peering around the room, there is no doubt that the place is beautiful. It is full of antique furniture and enormous windows with thick, dark wooden frames. It should feel warm and full of character, but it has no soul. The staff here walk around the place like they are afraid to speak. Nobody ever calls my father by his name, referring to him as Sir or Boss. There are at least a half a dozen bedrooms, but only two are occupied as far as I can tell — mine and my father's.

Every day dozens of Bratva men come here and meet with him, leading me to suspect he is high up in the organization. I should be doing something more. I should be finding the Wolf. But my father refuses to allow me into any of his meetings or to share any of the information he's learned about the elusive assassin during these past years. I mean, if he was aware the Ryan brothers were reaching out to the Wolf to hand me back, then he must have heard some whispers about where he might be.

Thoughts of the brothers bring a lump to my throat. I swallow a mouthful of soup as tears prick at my eyes. I am so lonely here, yet, I never felt lonely in their huge penthouse. From the moment I arrived, they made me feel welcome. Why would they let me get so close if they were just using me? It makes no sense.

I place my spoon on the table as a wave of tiredness washes over me. I can't seem to think straight lately. I need to shake whatever bug it is I'm coming down with so I can refocus on finding the man who slaughtered our family — with or without my father's help.

CHAPTER 4

CONOR

*L*iam kills the engine of the SUV as we pull up in the side street opposite Alexei Ivanov's mansion in Connecticut. From the outside, it looks like a fortress, but thanks to Shane's contacts in the State department, we've managed to get our hands on a copy of the original blueprints of the property. Blueprints that reveal the hidden passageways that were made when the house was first built back in the 1920s.

"Are you sure we shouldn't just blow the gates off and fight our way through there?" Mikey asks as he peers out of the window into the darkness.

"No," Shane replies with a look of warning at our younger brother. "We need to do this with as little noise and disruption as possible."

"But you don't where she is. Or if she's even in there?" Mikey sighs. He's annoyed that he has to wait in the car and can't get in on the action.

"Which is exactly why we don't need to be drawing any attention to ourselves," Shane snaps. "If she's not there..." He doesn't finish the sentence and I know it's because he can't bear to. He is as desperate to get Jessie back as we are, and although I imagine some of his motives are the same as ours, I recognize that he also wants revenge. He has a murderous look in his eyes that makes the hairs on the back of my neck stand on end.

"So, we wait here while you two break in, find Jessie, knock her out and bring her back to the car through one of the secret passageways?" Liam asks, doing what he does best and trying to diffuse the growing tension in the car.

"Do we really have to knock her out?" I groan.

"Yes!" Shane snarls. "How else are we going to get her out of there quietly? She went there willingly, remember? I doubt she's going to be thrilled to see us. It's not like we're putting her in a chokehold. A quick scratch and she'll fall asleep in your arms," he says with a roll of his eyes.

"If we hear shots fired, we're coming in there," Mikey grumbles.

"Fair enough," Shane nods his agreement.

"Let's fucking do this then," I say as I open the door of the car. Despite everything, I am eager to get in there. I want to see her face. I want to bring our girl home, whether she wants to come with us or not.

Shane climbs out behind me and hands me a gun with a silencer on the end, and I tuck it into the back of my jeans. We don't plan on using shooters, but it's better to be prepared, because we have no idea what we'll be facing once we get inside.

As we pull up the hoods of our black sweatshirts, we take a quick glance around us before jogging across the road to the small side gate that seems to double as the service entrance. It's always manned by two armed guards. Shane and I approach from the East, hoping to appear like two guys out for an evening jog. The guards are talking quietly and smoking cigarettes, but they straighten up as we approach.

We jog right on up, as though we're going to breeze past, and catch them both by surprise. I grab the bigger one, placing my hands around his neck and snapping it with ease. Shane does the same to his counterpart and the two men fall to the floor within a few seconds of each other. I hoist one of them up and rest his right thumb against the electronic keypad, and the metal gate clicks open. It's lazy security to use the thumb of your dominant hand on a fingerprint keypad system. It's the one that people always assume you'll use, and most people do.

"Let's get these two off the street," Shane says, and we drag their lifeless bodies through the entrance, dumping them just inside the walls as we close the gate behind us. I reach into my pocket and take out my knife before I lean down and cut off the thumb of the guy who just kindly opened the gate for us. It's a surgeon's blade and it slices easily through the bone and cartilage. I wipe the blood on my sweatshirt and pop his thumb into my pocket before handing the knife to Shane. "You may as well take his, too, in case we get split up?" I nod to the other dead man a few feet away.

"He was right-handed, wasn't he?" Shane asks as he holds the blade against the dead man's hand.

I nod and watch as my brother slices through his thumb and pockets it before we make our way toward the house. Another guard is patrolling just a few meters in front of us. Shane gives a low whistle, making him look in his direction and temporarily distracting him while I sneak up behind him and snap his neck, gently lowering him to the floor before pulling him into the nearby bushes. Snapping necks is my favorite way to kill someone. It's so quick and clean. It's a skill I learned at a very young age and one that I have continued to perfect ever since.

Once we're inside the house, we make our way upstairs and walk along the dim hallway, past the bedrooms, sure that Jessie must be in one of them. But there are at least six doors on this floor.

"You start at this end, and I'll start at the other," Shane whispers, and I nod my agreement. He walks to the other end of the hallway while I try the first door. The handle turns quietly, and I peer inside the dark room. It's a bedroom, but it doesn't appear to be occupied. I look up as Shane does the same at the opposite end of the corridor before looking at me and shaking his head.

Two down. Four to go.

I move along to the next room and grab hold of the handle, and I'm just about to turn it when it moves in my hand.

Shit!

I step back into the shadows as the door swings open, ready to go for my gun if I need to. Then she walks out of the bedroom and I swear my heart stops beating in my chest. She looks like Jessie, but not like her. Like maybe she's sleepwalking or something. Her beautiful red hair is tied up in a messy ponytail and she wears a nightdress which has a food stain on the front.

I step toward her and her eyes dart to the shadows where I'm standing. "Jessie," I whisper, unable to stop myself from reaching out to her. I'm vaguely aware of Shane making his way toward us. At first, she seems to stare right through me. But then I see the flicker of recognition in her eyes and her face suddenly becomes more animated.

"Con-" she starts to say my name before she falls backwards into Shane's arms and I realize he's injected the sedative into her neck.

"Let's get her out of here before someone notices us," Shane hisses.

I stand frozen to the spot as I stare at her, unconscious in his arms. There was something definitely not right about her.

"Conor!" Shane hisses through clenched teeth, snapping me from my momentary trance.

"We need to make sure there's no-one in that room waiting for her to come back in," I warn him.

He closes his eyes, as though the thought of someone being in there, in her bed with her soft warm body pressed up against them, pains him. I know that it fucking hurts me. I realize that if I look inside that room and see anyone in there, I will shoot him in the head. I don't give a fuck if we're supposed to be keeping this low key.

"Go on," he eventually replies with a flick of his head toward the door.

I walk closer to the room she has just walked out of. My heart is hammering in my chest now and the blood pounds against my eardrums. I open the door wider. Reaching inside, I flick on the light switch. The bed is empty. Rumpled covers confirm she was sleeping there, but she was alone. I sigh deeply and lean my forehead against the door frame. "It's clear. Let's go," I whisper as I turn around. "You want me to take her?" I offer.

"No, she hardly weighs anything," Shane replies as he hoists her up into his arms. I lift her arm and drape it around his neck, letting my hand linger on the skin of her wrist just a little longer than necessary. She's cold to the touch, despite this house being warm. My gut tells me there is something definitely not right here. That woman I just saw was definitely Jessie, but not the Jessie I've come to know.

DESPITE THE SECURITY in Alexei's fortress, Shane and I manage to make it out through one of the tunnels leading from the cellar without any further interference. We run over to the SUV as Mikey climbs out and opens the door to the back seat.

"She okay?" he asks as we approach.

"She's fine," Shane replies.

I jump in first and Shane places Jessie on the seat beside me. I pull her against me as he climbs in and Mikey runs back around to the front of the car. I lay Jessie's head on my lap as Shane pulls her feet onto his knees.

"Let's get moving," he barks to Liam, who puts the car into gear and pulls away from the curbside.

As I look at her, my heart feels like it constricts in my chest. I brush the hair back from her face. She looks so fucking peaceful lying here, but I know that when she wakes up, there will be no peace for her. Not for a while.

Whatever reason she had for leaving us, I doubt it's drastically changed in the space of four days. Shane is determined to make her talk, and I have no idea how he intends to do that, but I do know that he's had the dingy cell in the basement prepared for her. It's as small as a prison cell, but less comfortable. No natural light. A tiny metal bed screwed to the floor with a thin, bare mattress and a tiny stainless steel toilet in the corner.

We've kept plenty of people prisoner there before, but none that have ever got under our skin like this pint-sized little redhead lying on my lap.

So many emotions flood my senses that I don't know what I'm feeling. Relief at having her back with me. Fear of what she might tell us, or of what lengths we might go to make her talk. Anger that she left us. Jealousy that she might be in love with that man she left with or that she might be loyal to him in a way that she never was to us. And hope that, somehow, she has a perfectly reasonable explanation for everything and that it will piece my shattered heart back together.

I curl my fingers around her hair. Damn, Jessie! How the hell are we all going to get out of this in one piece?

CHAPTER 5

CONOR

*M*ikey paces up and down the concrete basement while Liam stares at the heavy metal door, rocking back on his heels and rubbing his hand over the stubble on his jaw.

"What the fuck do we do now?" Liam eventually asks and I look to Shane, who is leaning against the wall beside the door with his arms crossed over his chest.

"Now we wait," he replies with a shrug, as though it's just some person who means nothing to us who we've just locked in that tiny room and not Jessie.

"One of us should be in there with her when she wakes up," I snap at him. "She won't have a clue where she is once those drugs wear off."

"Well then, maybe she'll have some time to think about the fact that she betrayed us," Shane snarls at me.

"We don't know why she left," I remind him as I walk over to him.

"No! But she's going to fucking tell us. One way or another, isn't she?"

I step closer to him. "And just what the fuck does that mean, Shane?"

He edges toward me, pressing his face closer to mine. "It means that she is going to talk, Conor. And I will cross any line I have to in order to make that happen!"

"But that's Jessie in there!"

"Yeah? The same woman who promised us she would never leave, only to walk out of here holding some cunt's hand after leaving us a shitty note!" He snarls. "That Jessie? She's a fucking snake, and she fucked us all over, and we were all too fucking pussy drunk to see it," he rages.

I shake my head in exasperation. I know there's logic in what he's saying, but I don't want to accept it's true. Turning, I look at Mikey and Liam. They've always believed in Jessie just as much as I have. They both stare at me without speaking.

"Liam?" I say when I can't bear the silence any longer.

"I don't know, bro," he says with a shrug. "Shane has a point. You saw her walking out of here."

I suck in a breath. Of all people, I figured he might back me up.

"Mikey?" I try.

"Hey, we're not saying there isn't a possibility she has a good explanation for what she did, but right now, it's not looking likely, is it?"

"For fuck's sake!" I hiss.

"Conor!" Shane snaps. "You saw that house. The room she was staying in. She was a fucking guest there, not a prisoner! Whatever her reasons, she left willingly. There is no escaping that fact."

I look up into my older brother's face. I have always trusted his judgment and I accept there's every chance he's right about this. But I can't let myself believe that she lied to me, to all of us, because I don't think I can take it. And I fear what I might do to her if she tells me that Shane speaks the truth. I'm scared of what Shane, or any of us, might do to her.

25

"I'll wait down here. I'll check on her, and when she wakes up…" Shane offers.

"You'll what?" I ask with a frown.

"I'll speak to her. I won't hurt her. Promise. Not unless she attacks me first, anyway."

"Then I'll stay here. I'll talk to her!" I protest.

Shane stares at me as though I have just asked him to give me his kidney. In fact, he'd probably be more receptive to giving me one of his vital organs. "Fuck no! Not a chance!"

"Why not?"

"Because you can't be trusted around her."

"What?" I scowl at him, but he carries on.

"None of you can. She makes you all think with your dicks. I'd give it ten minutes before one of you either fucks her or lets her go!"

Liam and Mikey nod their agreement, but I slam my fist against the door beside his head. "So you're saying you don't trust me?" I snarl.

"Around Jessie? No," he snarls back.

"Well, maybe I don't trust you!"

"I'm the only one willing to do what needs to be done and you know it, Conor."

"And that's what I'm worried about. You're not thinking straight either, Shane. You're convinced she's betrayed us and you're not even willing to consider an alternative."

"Well, neither of you can go in there if you're at each other's throats," Liam says calmly from behind us.

"Exactly. So, you three go up to the apartment and I'll wait down here," Shane says to him over my shoulder. "And I'll let you know what she says when she's awake. I won't lay a finger on her."

"Okay," Liam replies. "You okay with that, Con?" He asks, placing a hand on my shoulder. My youngest brother has a way of bringing calm to a situation that I've never quite been able to fathom. Perhaps it's something in the tone of his voice, but something about him taps into something in us in a way that no-one else can.

"Whatever," I snap, because Shane is right. I'm not sure I trust myself around Jessie either.

"Good." Shane smiles at me reassuringly and I trust that he won't let anything happen to her. At least not yet.

CHAPTER 6

JESSIE

*G*roaning, I roll onto my side. My pulse throbs in my temples and my mouth is so dry I can barely swallow. Suddenly an image of Conor's face flashes into my mind. He was here. In my father's house. Someone was with him. The last thing I remember is the expression on Conor's face as a hand clamped around my mouth.

My eyes snap open. Where the hell am I? The room is tiny and dim. There are no windows. A small stainless steel toilet sits in one corner, about three feet away from the bed I'm lying on, which is nothing more than a bare mattress on a steel frame. My heart races in my chest, hammering against my ribcage as I sit up and try to get my bearings.

"About fucking time. I was beginning to think you'd never wake up," I hear a familiar voice growl from a dark corner. I spin my head toward the sound, noting the enormous steel door blocking the exit.

"Shane?" I croak, my voice hoarse from lack of fluids. How long have I been here? "Where am I?"

"Who are you working for, Jessie?" he snarls.

I blink at him as the memory of his hand over my mouth fills my senses. That was him in my father's house with Conor. Of course it was. I would recognize the touch of his skin on mine anywhere. "Did you drug me?"

"Who are you working for?" he repeats.

"Where am I, Shane? What the hell is going on?" I demand, but the tremor in my voice is audible. "Is the Wolf here?" I gasp as my eyes dart around the small space.

"Don't try and fuck with me," he snarls. "I asked you a fucking question."

I turn back to him. "And I asked you some too! And you won't get another word from me until you answer them." I glare at him.

He stands quickly, pushing the chair he was sitting on against the wall, and I flinch, scooting back along the bed. He stands before me, bending low and leaning his face close to mine before wrapping one of his powerful hands around my throat. "Do not fucking test me, Jessie, or I will snap your neck like a twig."

I stare into his eyes, that are so dark they no longer appear green at all. Silently, I challenge him to do it. I've had enough of this shit to last me a lifetime. Will I ever not be at the mercy of men like him? How fucking ironic that just a few days earlier, I completely believed him when he told me that he loved me.

"Do you have any idea what you did to them when you walked out of here with him?" he spits, his face and his voice so full of venom, I shrink back from him. Why is he pretending my leaving hurt them? Like they weren't planning on betraying me all along. Where are his brothers, anyway? Don't they have the guts to face me after what they were planning?

Shane tightens his hand on my throat and I close my eyes and wait for him to do his worst. I am so damn tired of it all. A few seconds later, he releases his grip and pushes me back until I am lying flat on the bed. I lie still and listen to his footsteps crossing the room before he opens the steel door and slams it closed behind him. I listen to the silence for a while, making sure that he has really gone before I open my eyes.

CHAPTER 7

LIAM

*A*s Mikey keeps himself busy cooking, Conor paces up and down the kitchen. He sits every few minutes and pulls out his cell phone, trying to focus on something, but it doesn't last long. Tension weighs heavy in the room as we wait for news from Shane.

"She must be awake by now," Conor barks.

"I'm sure Shane will let us know as soon as she is," I say.

"You think?" Conor pushes his chair back and walks toward the refrigerator and takes out a beer. Twisting off the cap, he throws it into the trash.

"He's not going to hurt her, Con. He's not going to do anything without discussing it first. You know that." I frown at him.

"But he's not thinking straight, Liam. You've seen how he's been these last few days. He's so fucking furious with her. What if..." Conor takes a long swig of his beer and then walks toward the window and looks out at the New York skyline.

I look across at Mikey who simply shrugs his shoulders and goes back to cooking. I can't remember a time in recent years when Shane and Conor have been so at odds. They are usually on the same page about everything and them being on opposing sides on an issue upsets the whole equilibrium of our existence.

Shane is the boss. That is an undeniable and unquestionable fact. Conor is his second.

Mikey and I enjoy being the ones who don't have to make the difficult decisions, because we are never made to feel like we are anything but equal partners when it comes to our business. I trust both of my older brothers to do a better job of it than either me or my twin can, so it makes me uneasy when they're not acting like the cohesive team they usually are.

Mikey will often jokingly refer to them as the folks, and I see what he means. If I had any happy memories at all of my parents or my childhood, I suppose I might compare this situation to the feeling kids must get when their mom and dad argue.

I walk across the kitchen and stand next to Conor. "Why are you fighting him so much on this?"

He turns to me with a scowl. "Why aren't you?"

"She left us, Conor. After everything she promised us. After everything we said to her. She just fucking upped and left."

His face softens and he turns back to the window. "She must have had a reason, Liam."

"I hope she fucking did. And who knows? Maybe she's down there explaining everything to him right now?"

Conor snorts and takes another drink of his beer.

"You know what it took for him to let her in, Con. You saw how happy she made him. And you know people only get one chance with him. I don't see how he's going to get past this."

"I know," Conor says with a sigh as he hangs his head low. "That's what I don't get, Liam. She worked so hard to get through to him. When she finally did, she was so fucking happy. That morning before she left, she was smiling. She looked at us like we were her whole fucking world. So, if that wasn't true, what was her game plan?"

"She left the day we put her fingerprints in the security system. That can't be a coincidence, Con."

He shakes his head. "But you saw how good she is, Liam. As sophisticated as our security system is, she could have hacked it in a day."

I put a hand on his shoulder and don't know how to answer that because he has a point. "So what could it have been then?"

"I don't know," he sighs. "But there must be some reasonable explanation, because if there isn't, what? She sucked us all in and made us fall in love with her for what? Plain old cruelty? I can't believe that."

I stare at my older brother and see the pain in his face. I understand the place he's coming from and the need to believe that Jessie is still the same person we thought she was. But what if she's not? "What if she doesn't have an explanation, Con? Have you even considered that? What are you going to do?"

He turns to me again and that haunted look in his eyes, the one I hoped I'd never see again, is back. "Of course I've considered it. But I can't think about what I'm going to do because it fucking terrifies me. I'm terrified of what he'll do to her. Of what I might do to her, Liam."

I swallow. I have no answers for him. I only hope that Jessie does. But I can offer him something. "I promise I won't let you do anything that you'll hate yourself for. Okay?" I wrap an arm around his neck and pull him to me.

"Yeah," he sighs.

"You two ready for some food?" Mikey shouts across the kitchen, interrupting the moment.

"I'm not hungry," Conor shouts back.

"What? I just spent an hour making this. And it's your favorite. You gotta eat, Con," Mikey snaps.

"Man has a point," I add.

"Fine," he snaps as he downs the last of his beer.

We're heading over to the table when Shane walks into the

33

room and we all look up at him expectantly. My eyes scan his face and his body, looking for any clues as to what might have happened downstairs. He's not covered in blood, so there's that.

"Is she awake?" Conor asks.

"Yeah," Shane says with a nod as he crosses the room to sit at the table.

"And?" I ask.

"She won't talk," he snaps.

"She didn't say anything?" Conor frowns at him.

"She played dumb. Wouldn't tell me who she was working for. And then she said some shit about the Wolf being here."

"The Wolf?" Conor interrupts him.

"Yeah," Shane says nonchalantly as he looks over at Mikey. "What's for dinner?" he asks.

Conor's entire body vibrates with anger. "Forget about dinner. What the hell did she say about the Wolf?" he shouts.

Shane turns to him and glares at him so fiercely, I almost shit my pants. I haven't seen him look at any of us like that since we were kids. "She asked if he was here. She is playing the victim card, Conor," he snarls. "Trying to make us feel sorry for her. She's probably been fucking the Wolf all along."

"Fuck you, Shane!" Conor snarls as he slams his fist on the table. Shane pushes his chair back, planting his hands on the table and leaning toward Conor as the two of them glare at each other, making the tension in the room ratchet up from uncomfortable to downright fucking unbearable. I feel like the kid in the middle of a bitter divorce here.

Against my better judgment, I stand by the center of the table and place a hand on each of their arms. "She's probably still confused by the drugs we gave her. Why don't we all have something to eat and then one of us can talk to her again?"

"I'll be the only one doing the talking," Shane snaps.

"And no-one is going to argue with that. So can you calm the fuck down and sit," I say to Shane before I turn to Conor who is practically foaming at the mouth. It fucking kills me to see my brothers like this. Damn, Jessie, better have a fucking good reason for putting us all through this shit. "Con. Let's sit down and eat, yeah?"

It takes a few seconds but the two of them back down and sit at the table and with impeccable timing, Mikey brings a huge bowl of chili to the table. Hopefully, he's made his extra special recipe that is so freaking hot, none of us will be able to talk much at all after a few mouthfuls.

CHAPTER 8

JESSIE

I have no sense of how long I've been in this tiny cell. I suspect it's in the basement of the brothers' building because I hear the bass thumping from the club upstairs occasionally. Since I've been here, I have mostly slept, no doubt because the bastards drugged me but, surprisingly, my head seems clearer now than it has in days.

As I look down at the floor, I notice there is a bottle of water and a pre-packed sandwich on a tray beside the bed. Shane must have brought it in, because he is the only person I've seen since I arrived here. Once after I first woke up, and a few more times when he has stood near the doorway and fired questions at me for what has felt like hours. Each time I have refused to answer any of them until he answered some of mine. And it seems like he is the only person I'll have an opportunity to ask, as clearly his brothers don't have the balls to face me.

The rattling of the door handle makes me glance up just in time to see the enormous piece of steel swing open. Once again, it's Shane who walks into the room and I scowl at him as soon as I see his face.

"Why the hell are you keeping me locked in here?" I snarl at him.

He kicks the door closed behind him and then he stalks toward me. "You know why," he growls at me. "Because you're a liar and I don't trust you."

"I'm a liar? That's rich coming from you."

His nostrils flare as he advances toward me while anger radiates from him like heat from a furnace. "Don't fucking push me!" he snarls.

I jump off the bed and square up to him, standing up onto my tiptoes so I can push my face as close to his as possible. "Or what, Shane?" I snap.

He wraps one of his huge hands around my throat. "Do you assume because I used to fuck you, that I won't snap your neck, Jessica?" he hisses.

"Oh, I know that you wouldn't. I'm not much use to you dead, am I?"

"You're no use to me alive right now, either. So, tell me what I want to know or I will leave you to rot in this filthy room for the rest of your days."

He says it with such conviction that I believe him. Suddenly, the prospect of spending the rest of my life in this tiny cell while they wait to hand me over to the Wolf fills me with anger and terror.

"Just let me go, Shane. Please?" I beg as he tightens his grip on my throat. "If you feel anything at all…"

My words seem to flip a switch in him and his green eyes darken until they are as black as coal. "Don't you fucking dare!" he hisses. "You think I could ever feel anything but hatred for you after what you did?"

After what I did? Is he for real? I take a deep breath as I realize I am running out of options fast and I have no choice but to use the only weapon I have available. I stare into his eyes and press my body closer to his. He is semi-hard and I'm relieved that at least one part of him responds to me the way it always has. "Seems like some part of you feels something," I purr at him as his growing erection presses against my abdomen.

"Just because my cock remembers what it was like to be buried in your cunt, doesn't mean I feel anything for you. I've fucked plenty of people I didn't like."

"Me too!" I narrow my eyes at him and, as much as I despise him right now, my body remembers all too well exactly how good he used to make me feel. How he convinced me he loved me.

"I don't doubt it," he spits. "Because you're a lying fucking whore!"

He releases his grip on my throat, and I lunge for him, clawing at his face. I scratch his lip but he grabs my wrists before I can do any real damage, spinning me around and pushing me toward the wall until I am pinned to it by the weight of his large frame. I feel his cock nudging at my ass and stifle a groan. The closeness of him makes my legs tremble and the smell of him and the sensation of his fingers on my skin floods my senses, causing wet heat to start to pool between my thighs.

"I bet you're wet right now," he growls in my ear. "Because you'll take any cock that's available. Won't you?"

His hand reaches beneath my nightdress and I draw in a breath. "No. Shane, don't," I breathe, because he is going to find me ready for him and I can't bear for him to realize that my body still reacts to his this way. He tugs my panties to one side and slides his fingers through my slick folds. "Soaking!" he hisses against my ear. "You want my cock, don't you?"

"Fuck you!" I half hiss, half groan as his fingers slide over my clit and he rubs firmly.

"Do you remember how hard you used to come for me?" he sneers.

"I faked it all!"

He chuckles against my skin. "Even you aren't that good,

Jessica. I'm going to make you come right now. Right here. All over my cock. And you're going to hate me for it."

He releases my wrists and I hear the familiar sound of his belt and zipper opening that makes a shiver of pleasure and anticipation skitter up my spine. This would be my chance to elbow him in the nuts and run. But I want this. I want to feel something. I want to feel him. I want to hate him so much, but my body is on fire for him. So I stand here, panting for breath and waiting for him to fuck me. A few seconds later, he pulls up my nightdress, fisting his hands in my panties and tearing them roughly over my skin before tossing the shredded material onto the floor. Then he bends his knees and pushes himself inside me, making my walls clench around him.

"Fuck!" he hisses against my neck. "Your cunt does love my cock, Hacker."

I bite down on my lip to stifle a moan as he nails me to the wall while his hand reaches around and rubs my clit, making my entire body thrum with heat and energy. Our breathing is hoarse and ragged. Our bodies bead with perspiration in the small, stuffy room. I bite the inside of my cheek as familiar waves of pleasure begin building in my core. Damn him and his huge cock. Despite how much I want to cry out, I clamp my mouth shut. I refuse to give him the satisfaction of hearing me come.

He realizes I'm on the edge and I hate that he knows my body so well. "Say my name," he growls as he runs his teeth along the delicate skin of my neck, making tremors of pleasure vibrate through me.

"No!" I hiss.

He pushes in deeper, rubbing at the sweet spot deep inside me, and making my legs tremble violently. "Say. My. Name," he orders, thrusting deeper into me with each word as his free hand reaches to one of my breasts and he kneads it roughly in his palm.

"Fuck you," I groan as he maintains his focus on those perfect spots.

"Say my name and I'll let you come."

I shake my head. I won't do it. I hate him.

Except I don't.

"Damn! Shane!" I groan and he sinks his teeth into my neck as he increases the pressure on all the places he is touching me until I come apart around him, trembling so much that he has to hold me upright.

My orgasm seems to send him over the edge too as he presses my body flush to the wall and fills me with his cum.

"Fuck, Jessie!" he hisses, and then he releases me, staggering backwards before zipping up his fly and buckling his belt.

I turn around and watch him. There are so many emotions raging through my body that I don't know which one to deal with. Stupidly, I hope for some sort of connection with him, but he doesn't even look at me. That can't have meant nothing. Two bodies don't do that together without there being something between them, do they?

But he doesn't glance my way again. Instead, he walks out of the room and closes the door behind him, tearing out my heart in the process. I have endured more pain and humiliation and torment in ten years than most people experience in a lifetime, but I have never felt so empty and worthless as I do right now.

I am nothing to him. I am nothing to anyone anymore. Even my father has changed so much from the man I knew. He wants a daughter who doesn't speak, doesn't question or challenge him in any way. One that will give him grandchildren and never cause him an ounce of trouble. And that is most definitely not me.

I slide down the wall until I'm sitting on the cold stone floor and start to sob quietly.

CHAPTER 9

SHANE

*M*y blood thunders around my body as I stumble through the door and pull it closed behind me. Pressing my forehead against the cold steel, I suck in a lungful of air.

What the fuck have I just done?

I convinced my brothers that they should let me deal with Jessie, because I don't trust them to keep their hands off her and, clearly, I can't either. Five minutes alone with her and I have my fingers and my cock inside her. And fuck, I wanted to throw her down on that bed and taste her too, and I know she would have let me.

Whatever has happened between us, her body still responds to mine the way it always has. I close my eyes as the memories of all the times I have eaten her sweet cunt overwhelm me. All the times she has moaned my name. The times she told me that she loved me. The times she looked me in the eyes and swore to me she would never leave us. And I believed her.

Liar!

My pulse races and my heart pounds as I try to steady my breathing. Jessica Romanov has a hold over me that I can't explain. Even though I want to hate her with everything I have, I can't fucking resist her. Running my tongue over my lower lip, I taste the blood from where she scratched me. Unconsciously, I lift my hand and brush two fingers over the small cut and instantly regret it because I taste her on me and the blood rushes straight back to my cock.

Why won't you just fucking talk to us, Jessie? Tell us this is all a huge misunderstanding so that I can fucking breathe again.

But she won't. Because she can't. She is a liar and a manipulator. And if she won't talk to me now, then I'm going to have to be a little harder on her.

Pushing myself back from the door, I walk back through the basement to the elevator. Conor is out of town for the night, which gives me the perfect opportunity to test Jessie's limits a little further, because he would never agree to what I'm about to suggest to the twins.

I FIND the twins in the kitchen. Mikey is making dinner while Liam sits at the island scrolling through his cell phone. They both glance up as I walk in and I wonder if they can see on my face what just happened downstairs. Or whether they will smell her on me if I get too close.

"How is she?" Liam asks, his eyes narrowed at me as though he knows what I've just done.

"Still not talking," I reply with a shrug as I walk to the refrigerator and take out a bottle of water.

"Shit! Still?" Mikey frowns before glancing at the stove. "Shall I make her some dinner?"

"No!" I say before taking a long drink of water. "If she refuses to talk, then perhaps we're being too nice?"

"Too nice? She's locked in a tiny room with nothing but a bed and a crapper. How exactly are we being nice?" Liam snaps.

"She's getting food and water. She's been here for two days

and I've given her plenty of opportunities to talk to me. Perhaps what she needs is a little time to herself?"

"What are you suggesting?" Mikey says.

"Twenty-four hours on her own to think about where she is, what's she's done, and how her only way out is to talk to us."

"With no food or water?" Liam asks.

I shake my head in response.

"Fuck, Shane!" he hisses.

"It's one day, Liam. She's got some water down there and she's not going to starve."

"Conor wouldn't be happy about this," Mikey says with a low whistle and a flash of his eyebrows.

"Well, Conor's not here. Besides, last time I checked, I was the one in charge around here."

"She's going to hate us for leaving her like that," Liam says with a shake of his head.

"She already hates us, kid," I remind him before I turn back to Mikey. "What time is dinner?"

"Twenty minutes," he replies.

"Good. I'll be back in twenty then. I need to take a shower," I say, not giving them a chance to ask me why. I need to wash her scent off me because it is driving me fucking crazy.

The last thing I want to do is leave Jessie down there all alone. I would much rather bring her up here, tie her to my bed, and keep her there forever. But I don't trust myself not to fall for her lies again. And if she didn't get to me, then she would get to one of my brothers instead. Because we all think with our dicks around her.

I tell myself that, but the truth is so much more devastating. We all gave her our hearts. We gave her everything and she threw it in our faces. And no matter what excuse she comes up with, whatever lies she might tell to convince my brothers, I will never forgive her for it.

CHAPTER 10

JESSIE

*I*t seems like it's been a few hours since Shane left and the cramps in my stomach started shortly after. At first I wondered if they were brought on by the sex. Not that it was particularly rough, at least not by Shane's standards, but they have been growing stronger and stronger. I groan loudly as I feel the warm, sticky wetness between my legs and realize my period has started a few days early and has chosen to arrive at the worst possible time. I don't even have any damn panties since Shane tore them off me. Just this stupid nightdress. Not even a sheet on the bed to soak up the blood. I can't just sit on that awful uncomfortable toilet until he or one of his brothers decides I'm worthy of another visit.

I cross the room and bang on the door with my fists. "Hey. I need to speak to one of you," I shout.

No answer.

"Hey. Please? I need some things. I'm bleeding here."

Still no answer. Damn! I don't even know if any of them are out there.

I go on banging on the door, yelling until my voice is hoarse and my knuckles are bruised. No-one is coming. I'm bleeding heavily now and there's not a damn thing I can do to stem the flow. I crawl over to the mattress and lie down, curling into a ball as I start to cry again. Never in my whole life have I felt so alone. Knowing that the men I once felt so loved by are out there letting me suffer like this is so painful to me that all I want to do is fall asleep and never wake up.

WAKING WITH A START, I shiver in the cold room. My bottom half is soaked and sticky. I have no idea how long I've been lying on this mattress. I must have fallen asleep and now everything is soaked in my blood. My eyes and throat are raw from crying. I feel so weak I don't think I can stand even if I wanted to.

I don't have the energy to look up when the door opens.

"Oh fuck, Red," I hear someone say and assume it's Mikey because that was what he used to call me.

Someone else walks into the room then. "What the fuck!" he hisses and I realize it's Conor and my heart almost breaks in two. I hear mumbling between the two of them, but I can't make out what they're saying and I no longer care. The Ryan brothers can all go to hell.

I have a sudden sense of movement and my eyes snap open as I realize Conor has lifted me off the bed. I try to recoil from him, but his arms are huge and I am wrapped in them. "Get your hands off me!" I can only croak the words because my voice is so damn hoarse from screaming and shouting for help.

"I'm not going to hurt you, Jessie," he says softly, "but we need to get you cleaned up."

I don't have the strength to fight him, so instead I close my eyes and wait for whatever fresh hell is in store for me next. I can smell gasoline and fresh air as he walks me through the basement and toward the elevator before he steps inside. A few moments later, I hear the ping of the door opening, signaling we've arrived at wherever he's taking me.

"What the fuck?" I hear Shane's voice saying from nearby and Conor's arms tense around me, but I still don't open my eyes.

"Stay the hell away from her, Shane," Conor growls. "She is not going back to that fucking basement."

I can't help but feeling a small surge of relief at that, because I hate that freaking basement. But it's a small comfort. So what if they keep me in luxury? They're still planning on handing me back to the Wolf.

Conor keeps on carrying me through the apartment and I open my eyes to find we are in my former bedroom. I choke back a sob as I recall the memories we have shared in this room. And despite everything, being wrapped in Conor's strong arms is so warm and familiar.

Mikey comes out of the bathroom as we head toward it. "Tub is running. I used some of that vanilla stuff you like, Red," he says with a half-smile and my stupid face smiles back instinctively.

"Can you stand?" Conor asks.

"Yes."

He places me down on my feet and then holds his arms out around me as though I'm a child who is just learning to walk.

"I'm fine," I snap. "It's just my period. But I had nothing down there to stop it…" I shake my head and swallow the tears.

"I know. I'm sorry," Conor whispers.

"I'm going to leave you to it," Mikey says with a final anxious glance at me before he walks out of the room.

My head spins and I place my hand on the wall to steady myself, leaving bloody fingerprints on the pristine paintwork.

"You sure you're okay?" Conor asks.

I look up into his face, the one that I used to love so much. No, I'm not okay, Conor. You and your brothers have kidnapped me and left me to rot in some windowless, airless room, you bunch of heartless assholes! That's what I want to say, but instead I simply nod.

His Adam's apple bobs in his throat as he swallows, and I

notice that his expensive gray suit is covered in my blood. Nice! Serves him right for leaving me with no sanitary products. "All of your things are still here. You can stay in this room now. I'll bring you some food in a little while."

I nod at him. "I should get cleaned up."

"Yeah. Of course."

"You wouldn't want me looking a mess when you hand me over to the Wolf, would you?" I snap and he frowns at me, but I don't give him a chance to reply. I turn and walk into the bathroom, locking the door behind me.

CHAPTER 11

CONOR

*C*losing the door to Jessie's bedroom, I walk through the apartment to Shane's office. My head is spinning with questions. I'm pretty sure Jessie just accused me of wanting to hand her over to the Wolf, but right now I'm so fucking angry, I can't process any rational thoughts.

Walking inside Shane's office, I slam the door behind me. I didn't imagine I could be any angrier than I was thirty minutes ago when I came home to find he had left her down in that shit-box room without even checking on her for almost twenty fucking hours. But then I found her like that. And when I saw the blood, I thought she had really hurt herself and my world stopped turning. It was only as I was lifting her into my arms, I realized she had got her period and I have never been so relieved in my entire life.

Shane looks up and glares at me as I stride over to his desk. "Did you fuck her?" I snarl.

He continues glaring at me, his jaw set and a vein throbbing in his temple, but I clearly saw the pair of torn panties in that room downstairs. I'm pretty sure Jessie didn't rip them off herself.

"Did you fuck her?" I shout this time.

"Yes," he snaps, and I have to stop myself from jumping over his desk and punching him in the mouth.

"So, it's just me and the twins who have to keep away from her, is that it? But you can fuck her whenever you feel like it?"

"It just happened," he snaps, his eyes narrowed at me in anger.

"Seriously? You just fell into her?"

"You know what I mean!"

"And you say I'm blinded by her. A few minutes in her company and you can't help but bury your dick in her? And was she even okay with it?"

"Of course she fucking was, Conor!" he snarls at me.

"What the fuck, Shane?" I snarl back. "How could you just fuck her and then leave her down there like that? How could you not check on her?"

"She's okay, isn't she? Liam told me she got her period. I didn't know she was bleeding. She was fine when I left her."

"But you left her for almost a whole fucking day and night, Shane. Anything could have happened to her. Why the fuck would you do that?"

"What the hell else was I supposed to do, Conor? She won't fucking talk. She's working for the Russian mob and she won't give us any answers. She's had every fucking opportunity to talk and she refuses to."

"You don't know that she's working for them," I remind him.

He shakes his head at me, the way he used to when I was fourteen years old and I'd come home drunk after staying out all night. "You are so fucking blind when it comes to her."

Planting my hands on his desk, I lean forward. "I'm blind?" I shout. "You refuse to consider any possibility other than her betraying us. There are other reasons why she might have left, but you won't listen to any of them."

He stands up and leans forward too. "She was holding his fucking hand, Conor. She didn't look frightened or threatened or any of the other things you've suggested to me these past few days. In fact, she looked fucking thrilled to be walking out on us."

"You don't fucking know that though."

"No, I don't," he snarls. "And while she refuses to give us any explanation, I suppose my theory will just have to do, won't it? Maybe we'll never understand why she left. But I do know that she ripped out our fucking hearts, and I will never forgive her for that."

"So, what do you plan on doing with her, then?" I lean back, my arms crossed over my chest.

He shrugs. "Fuck knows."

"You know that we're going to have to let her go eventually?"

"What?" he frowns at me.

"If she doesn't want to be here, then what's the alternative, Shane? Because I'll be fucked if I'll let you hurt her any more than we already have, or send her back down to that basement."

"I want answers, Conor. She needs to explain herself. I need to understand why she left with him and what the hell she was doing here in the first place."

We're interrupted by a knock at the door and I turn around to see Liam opening it. "Doc is on her way," he says to Shane.

Shane nods in response.

"You called Lisa?" I ask him.

"I didn't know what was up with her until Liam told me. Probably best we get her checked over anyway," he shrugs.

"Yeah," I nod in agreement, and it's only then that I realize his anger is masking everything else he's feeling. The pain of losing her. The guilt at the state we've just found her in. Shane loves her just as much as I do, but he will never admit it. It's easier for him to pretend that he hates her. I wish I could hate her too. I wish I could let her walk out of here and be happy to never see her face again. But the thought of doing that makes me sick to my stomach. We need to find a solution to this nightmare we've ended up in. And soon.

CHAPTER 12

SHANE

I feel my brothers' eyes burning into me as we sit waiting for Lisa to finish checking Jessie over. When Conor walked out of the elevator with her and I saw her covered in blood, I swear my heart stopped beating. For a few awful moments, I thought she'd hurt herself, and that we would lose her for good. Conor was furious with me, and I couldn't blame him. It was Liam who started my heart again, whispering in my ear and telling me she had got her period. And because I'd left her in that room with nothing other than a bare mattress and a few sheets of tissue paper, she'd had nothing to soak up the bleeding.

As a precaution, I called Lisa and asked her to check Jessie over anyway. Perhaps it was a way of easing my guilt, although I would never admit that to anyone.

Lisa walks through to the kitchen and places her medical bag on the table with a heavy sigh.

"How is she?" Conor asks.

"She's sleeping now. It would do her good to get some rest," she replies, and the tone of her voice and the expression on her face are something I've never experienced before. Lisa knows what we do and she never judges — at least not usually.

"What is it?" I ask.

She swallows as she turns to face me. "Have you been giving her drugs?"

"We gave her a sedative three days ago when we brought her back here. Why?"

She narrows her eyes at me as though she's deciding whether to believe me.

"Why, Lisa?" I snap.

"I took a urine sample, and that girl has so many drugs in her system, I'm surprised she's able to function."

"Like what?" Conor snaps.

"Everything! She lit up my tox screening like a Christmas tree. Where the hell was she?"

"Nowhere you need to be concerned about. So, what are you telling us here?" I ask.

"Well, if you didn't give her them, someone else obviously did."

"So, she was being drugged?" Mikey asks.

"Or she took them herself?" I add.

"It's a strange combination to take yourself," Lisa says, shaking her head. "I never got any sense she was into drugs, did you?" She glances around at all four of us and my brothers shake their heads.

"That would explain why she's been talking crazy about the Wolf?" Conor says with a frown.

"That or being kidnapped and held in a cell with very little light and no idea of what was going to happen to her," Lisa snaps.

Conor closes his eyes as though he is deeply ashamed.

"You have no clue what's going on here, Doctor, so I suggest you tread carefully. Besides, you can't believe half of what comes out of Jessie's mouth," I say.

Lisa walks up to me and looks me in the eye. "That's just it. She didn't tell me shit. I'm aware of the room downstairs because

Mikey showed me where she'd been. I wanted to know how much blood she'd lost because when Conor showed me her clothes, I suspected a miscarriage."

"Miscarriage?" I frown and I swear I'm going to have a fucking heart attack if I get any more surprises today.

"It wasn't. Don't worry. Her HCG levels were normal," Lisa says and relief washes over me. "She suffers from incredibly heavy periods. But she told me nothing. In fact, she barely spoke. I can hardly believe it's the same woman I saw here five months ago."

"Well, a lot has happened since then."

"No shit! Physically, she is exhausted, but fine. Emotionally – not so much. I don't know what your game plan is here, but she is in a vulnerable state right now. She is terrified of something, but she won't tell me what. You need to tread carefully, Shane."

I nod my agreement and her face softens.

"I told her that she has nothing to fear from you. Please don't make me a liar," she places a warm hand on my arm and then she glances at her watch. "I have an appointment to get to. I'll call back in a few days and see how she is."

"Thanks, Lisa."

"Any time," she nods. "Bye, guys."

Liam escorts her to the elevator and we wait for his return before we discuss what Lisa just revealed. When he does, it's Conor who speaks first.

"So, Jessie was being drugged by whoever took her. And then we drugged her, kidnapped her, and left her alone in a tiny fucking cell?" he snarls.

"Nobody took her. You watched her on that video. You watched her stroll right out of here," I shout.

"Just because she held the guy's hand doesn't mean there wasn't something else going on," he shouts back.

"Then why won't she tell us what the hell is going on? That's all she has to do," I remind him.

Liam and Mikey sit down at the breakfast bar, knowing better than to get in the middle of anything between me and Conor.

"You heard Lisa. She is terrified. She was on a cocktail of fucking drugs. And then we drugged her and kidnapped her, Shane," he says again, as though I might have forgotten this information in the last twenty seconds. "She woke up in that tiny fucking cell and who knows what the fuck she was thinking. And you wonder why she wouldn't talk to you? Then you fucked her instead, before you left her to lie there for twenty fucking hours, shouting for help. Shouting for something so she wouldn't have to lie there bleeding all over herself."

"I didn't know that she was going to get her period, Conor."

"No. But you would have if you'd have fucking checked on her like we agreed. You're convinced that she's the enemy..."

"She walked out of here holding the hand of the head of the Russian fucking mob!" I stalk toward him, my face inches from his.

"You don't know that!" he hisses.

I don't even see Mikey or Liam move, but I feel Liam's hands on my shoulders. "This whole situation is fucked up," he says in that quiet tone he has that seems to tap into something in me that reminds me so much of our mother. "But, we can fix this, can't we? Let's give Jessie some time to rest and then we can talk to her tomorrow and straighten everything out."

Tension slips from my shoulders. I realize my anger is fueled by my guilt too. Perhaps I have been too harsh on Jessie. What if there is an explanation for what she did? But I can't forget the looks on my brothers' faces when they realized she had left us. I can't forget how my world ended when I read that note. She looked in my eyes and promised me she would never leave us, and like a goddamn fool, I believed her.

We made her family, and she walked out on us like we were nothing to her. I can admit I wanted to punish her for that. I don't believe in happy ever afters. To think that it might have been some sort of misunderstanding, and that everything she told us while she lived here wasn't a lie, is too hard. It's easier to be angry and blame her than to hope that she might come back to us.

"If she doesn't want to be here, then we have to let her go, Shane," Conor says quietly, "because the alternative is unthinkable."

I nod at him. I'll never forgive her, but I could never hurt her either. "I still want answers."

He places his hand on the back of my neck. "Then we'll get some. I promise."

CHAPTER 13

JESSIE

*M*y eyelids flutter awake at the sound of the door opening. I sit up quickly and rub my eyes, watching as Conor walks into the room and toward the bed.

"I'm sorry. I didn't mean to wake you. I just wondered if you needed anything else?" he asks softly, almost as though I'm his guest again and not his prisoner now.

"No. I'm good, thanks," I croak.

He looks at the uneaten sandwich and the unopened bottle of Gatorade on the nightstand and sighs. "You need to eat and drink, Jessie."

"I ate the candy. And I drank some water from the faucet. I'm fine."

"Why didn't you eat the sandwich? Or the Gatorade? Blue is your favorite."

I glare at him in the dim light of the room. "I couldn't be sure they weren't poisoned. The seal on the Gatorade was broken."

"Poisoned?" he snaps. "Dammit, Jessie. What the fuck?" He runs a hand over his beard and shakes his head.

"You knocked me out and kidnapped me, Conor!" I shout at him.

He sucks on his top lip and holds his hands up in surrender as he steps closer to the bed and then he stares at me with those deep, brown eyes. "How did we get here, Angel?"

"Don't call me that," I say, my voice cracking with emotion as tears prick at my eyes. "You don't get to call me that anymore."

He drops his head low and then he just stands there for a few moments. I watch his chest rise and fall with each breath he takes and all I can think about is how much I loved him. How much I still love him. My heart feels like it's breaking into a million pieces as he stands there right in front of me. Close enough to touch, but a million miles away.

"Get some rest, Jessie," he says eventually in a low growl that vibrates through my core.

"Why?" I snap.

He glares at me, his dark brown eyes smoldering as his jaw works while he tries to keep his temper in check. He probably came in here trying to be nice. As if he could get me back on side by pretending that he cares about me. Cashing in on the fact that he rescued me from that horrible cell in the basement. I swallow hard as I recall how good it was to be held in his arms a few hours ago. How the warmth of his body against mine still brings me comfort despite everything that's happened.

"Because I fucking told you to," he eventually snarls before turning around and walking through the open door.

I lie back against the pillows, unable to stop the tears rolling down my cheeks. I wish I knew how we'd ended up here too.

CHAPTER 14

JESSIE

The following morning, Conor and Liam come to my room to tell me that I'm wanted for a family meeting. Their family now, obviously, and no longer mine. I walk along the hallway behind Conor and with Liam trailing behind me. When we reach the dining room, Shane and Mikey sit at the table already waiting and I swallow as I glance around the room, recalling what happened the last time we were in here and we made our 'cum oath'. The night when I was officially welcomed into the family. What a crock of shit that turned out to be.

"Sit!" Shane orders as I reach the table and, like an obedient puppy dog, I do as I'm told.

Conor and Liam sit next to their brothers and the four of them stare at me like I'm at a job interview. I glare back at them. They don't intimidate me.

"Shall we just get this over with?" I snap.

Shane scowls and rubs a hand over his jaw and Mikey grins, but it's Conor who speaks.

"You want out of here, Jessie?" he asks.

"What do you think, asshole?"

"I told you this is not going to get us anywhere," Shane snarls.

"And like I said, what's our alternative?" Conor frowns at him and suddenly I'm wondering what that alternative is too. Are they just going to kill me after going to all of this trouble to keep me alive?

Shane turns back to me. "You can walk out of here today. But in order for us to allow that to happen, you're going to have to tell us the truth. Now, I appreciate that's like asking the rain not to fall, but you can manage it sometimes, right?"

"You keep talking about me lying to you, Shane, but I only ever lied about who I was when I first met you," I snarl at him. "You are the liar. All of you are."

He rolls his eyes while the other three frown at me.

"Who are you working for?" Shane asks.

"Nobody. I told you that."

"You're lying."

"I am not! Who the hell would I be working for? What do you think you have here, the codes for Fort Knox or something? So, you have money? Anyone can take your money if they want it bad enough. What the hell would I be doing here for months?"

"Then why were you holed up in the fortress of Alexei Ivanov? The head of the Russian mob?" Shane snaps.

I frown in confusion. Who the hell is Alexei Ivanov? "If that is his place, then I was just staying there with someone."

"Who?"

"None of your damn business."

"Really? Don't you think you owe us that much, Jessie?"

"Owe you? I owe you nothing. I have never done anything to harm any of you. I did the jobs you asked me to do. I never asked for anything from any of you. What we did... I never," I shake my head and don't finish the sentence because thinking about what we were is too painful.

"For fuck's sake, Jessie. You walk out of here with some Russian, holding his fucking hand. You won't tell us who he is and you expect us to believe that you weren't up to something?"

"I didn't even know he existed until that day."

Shane frowns. "What? You didn't know him, and you just strolled out of here holding his hand? You expect us to believe that?"

I shift in my seat. "I did know him a long time ago... It's complicated."

"Then uncomplicate it, Jessie, or I swear to God, I will put a bullet in your head right now," Shane snarls.

"How are you going to get your money from the Wolf then?" I challenge him.

"What the fuck are you on about?" he scowls at me.

I clamp my lips together and sit back in my chair as Conor leans forward in his. "Is he worth losing everything for, Jessie? Tell us who he is and why you went with him and you can walk out of here." He stares at me with those deep brown eyes and I remember all the times I looked into them and the love I felt. How did all of it come to mean nothing? Did it ever mean anything?

Suddenly, I am so tired of everything. I can't do this anymore. I have been fighting for so long, I'm exhausted by it. "You promise?"

"Yes."

I take a deep breath. I don't know who I trust or what I believe any longer, but what have I got to lose when I've already lost everything? "He's my father," I stammer.

All four of them stare at me with their mouths open.

"So, your father wasn't the guy who was killed by the Wolf?" Conor asks.

"Yes. But he didn't die. He survived."

"No. That's impossible. I saw the police reports. You're lying," Shane snaps.

"I appreciate that it seems impossible. But it's him. He managed to escape from our house that night and then there was some kind of coverup."

"Jessie!" Shane interrupts me. "You saw what the Wolf did to him. You've seen those police reports too. The autopsy reports. Your father is dead."

Tears prick at my eyes. "I know. But he was here. That day I came back from the salon, he was here. He said he'd been looking for me all this time." I sniff as I wipe the tears from my cheeks. "I know it sounds crazy, but it was him."

"But why did you go?" Conor asks. "Why didn't you wait for us?"

I swallow hard as I look at them. I suppose I'm all in now, anyway. "He told me that the reason he'd found me was because you were trying to reach out to the Wolf. So you could sell me back to him."

"And you believed him?" Conor snaps.

"He's my father!"

"No, he's not!" Shane interrupts me.

"You don't understand," I say with a shake of my head. "I thought he was dead. And then he was standing there. Right in front of me. I was in shock. I wasn't thinking clearly. And then he told me that was how he found me and I... I didn't have time to question him. He said we had to leave."

"Red," Mikey says. "You can't honestly think that we would do that?"

"Really? The four guys who kidnapped me and kept me in a cell for days with hardly any food or water?" I snap. "No. You would never do anything like that, would you?"

"But that was because we thought you were working for the Russians. We came home and you'd left that stupid fucking note. You didn't think we'd check the security feed and see you walking out of here holding some guy's hand? What the fuck did you expect us to do, Jessie?" Shane snaps.

I blink at him. I'm so damn confused. "I don't know," I look down at my hands. "But why would he lie to me? And how did he find me if it wasn't because of you?"

"The guy from Balthazar's," Conor says with a sigh. "He didn't die, Jessie. At least not for a few days. And he obviously recognized you as your mother's daughter. That must be how he found you."

"What?" I look up and blink at him, trying to process this newest piece of information.

Mikey whispers something to Shane who nods at whatever his brother said before he pushes a piece of paper across the desk to me. "These are the results of the urine tests the doc did on you yesterday. She double checked them in the lab and emailed these this morning. You see all of those drugs that were in your system?"

I reach for the paper and read over it. Barbiturates. Ketamine. PCP. Xanax. Some drugs that I can barely even pronounce or have ever heard of. I shake my head. "You gave me something," I frown.

"We gave you a fast acting sedative that wouldn't show up in any tests after forty-eight hours. That's why we use it."

"So?" I peer down the list. "Ketamine? That's a hallucinogenic, right?"

"Hallucinogens can also make you more susceptible to suggestion," Conor says.

"You're saying I've been drugged?"

"That's what the results say," Shane replies. "Unless you took them willingly?"

"I don't do drugs," I snap. "And besides, this could be falsified. How do I know I'm not drugged now and you're making this shit up to confuse me?"

Shane lets out a long breath and shakes his head. "Forget the drugs then. Why would we hand you over to the Wolf, Jessie? Discounting the fact that he has disappeared and nobody has a clue where he is, I offered you your freedom, remember? The car and the money and you told me to stick it up my ass."

I stare at him because I don't know how to respond. None of

this makes any sense. Except that it does, doesn't it? The zavarka in the car on the way to Connecticut. All of the tea and soup I was constantly given to make me feel better when I assumed I was coming down with the flu. Shit! The rational part of my brain is telling me that it all makes perfect sense, but I'm not ready to acknowledge it just yet.

"We put your fingerprints in our system. You weren't a fucking prisoner here. We made you one of us. Why the hell would we do any of that? And selling you? In case you haven't noticed, we've got plenty of money already," Shane snaps.

Tears run down my cheeks as my brain forces me to confront the reality of what has been going on for the past week.

"Did you think that everything we did and told you was a lie?" Conor asks.

I look up at him through tear-filled eyes. "Did you?" I sniff. "Because you were just as quick to assume I was working with the Russians."

He sits back in his chair and runs a hand over his jaw and all four of them stare at me as my world comes crashing down around my ears once again.

"All I know is my father was standing in front of me, asking me to go with him and telling me that I was in danger and you were betraying me. I was confused. I…" I shake my head. "I'm sorry."

"He's not your father, Jessie," Shane says again.

"Then who is he?" I say. "Because he looks just like him. He has the same voice. He even feels like him."

"Red," Mikey says softly and suddenly, the last piece of the puzzle falls into place.

"My brothers were twins." I put my head in my hands. "They run in my family and I still didn't think. I just saw his face. And he was so convincing. He swore he was my father."

"Perhaps he is?" Shane suggests. "Just not the one you know."

"So you're not planning to hand me over to the Wolf?"

"We're not planning on handing you over to anyone, Angel," Conor says, and my heart starts beating so quickly that it feels like it might burst out of my chest.

I sit there, blinking at them as tears stream down my face. I don't even know what to say or where to begin, but I don't have to, as the sound of an alarm pierces the air.

"Shit! We got company," Conor shouts as Liam and Mikey open the huge safe on the wall.

"Looks like your daddy has come to take you home, Hacker," Shane raises an eyebrow at me.

"Then you'd better give me one of those guns," I say as I wipe the tears from my face and nod toward the array of weapons that Mikey has started laying on the table.

"Not a chance," he shakes his head, but Liam tosses me one anyway and winks at his older brother.

"If she wanted to shoot you in the head, she'd have done it weeks ago," Liam grins.

"You know how to use that thing?" Conor asks.

"Sure do," I reply.

"This is fucking insane," Shane mutters under his breath.

As adrenaline courses around my body, I take a deep breath and tuck the gun into the back of my jeans, before following Conor and the twins out of the kitchen.

CHAPTER 15

SHANE

alf a dozen of our men are already in the club by the time we get down there and there are at least a dozen Russians too now, from what I can see. I wonder if Alexei Ivanov has come himself to get his daughter back. I certainly hope so because I want nothing more than to come face to face with him. There are shots being fired in every direction and Jessie is sandwiched between me and Conor as we edge into the club.

A gunshot whizzes past us and we dive for the cover of the bar as Liam and Mikey stride into the room like they're made of titanium. Mikey tosses two grenades into the middle of the club while Liam shoots anything that moves that isn't Irish or female. The Russians return the gunfire amid lots of shouting and noise while the twins head to the safety of the DJ booth.

We crouch behind the bar and I sense Jessie getting twitchy beside me. "Don't do anything stupid," I warn her before I turn to Conor. "I think the twins have taken a few of them out. I'm going to head out and come at them from the side. Cover me."

Conor nods, but before I can act on my plan, Jessie moves while I'm distracted. She stands up from behind the bar and holds her hands in the air. "Papa!" she shouts, and the gunfire stops.

I grab hold of her leg. "Get the fuck down. Now!" I snarl at her.

She looks down at me and shakes her head. She is the fiercest woman I have ever known and I admire her almost as much as I hate the fact that she refuses to do as she's told. "He's here for me. I won't have any of you getting hurt because of me."

"You are not leaving here with him, Jessie," Conor snaps.

"I need answers. I need to know who he really is. Please let me do this my way."

I rub a hand over my face and sigh. "Fine. Let her try."

Jessie gives me a brief smile and then she walks from behind the bar as Conor and I stand and train our guns on the men opposite us.

"Jessica. Idite syuda!" Come here!

"I'm here, Papa. But please ask your men to lower their weapons. I don't want my friends hurt."

"These men are not your friends," Alexei snarls. "Friends do not steal you away in the night."

"They didn't steal me. I came willingly," she lies.

There are a few moment's silence. "If they will lower theirs first," the reply eventually comes in a thick Russian accent.

I grind my teeth so hard my jaw aches, but I do as he asks. "Stand down," I shout around the room and my men do the same, but I know that Liam has a sniper rifle in that DJ booth and he will have it trained on Alexei.

The Russians lower their weapons and a tall man, who I assume is Alexei, appears from the shadows. He holds out his arms to her. "Why did you run away?"

"Because you lied to me," she says.

He shakes his head. "It is not I who is lying to you. It is these Irish pigs. They fill your pretty head with nonsense, printsessa.

And I will make every one of them suffer for taking you from me."

Conor bristles beside me, and I put my hand on his arm. We will have our chance as soon as Jessie is out of harm's way.

Jessie glances around the room. The Russians appear to outnumber us, but they don't have the upper hand. Jessie doesn't know how good Liam is with a sniper rifle. Or how Mikey has explosives stashed in a floor safe beneath the DJ booth.

I see the exact moment she falters. "Then I'll come back with you, Papa. Promise me you won't hurt my friends and I'll leave with you right now."

I frown at Conor. She knows what he did to her. She knows he is probably the man responsible for killing her family, but she would do that? For us? Or so that she can exact her revenge? Or both?

"I told you. These animals are no friends of yours, Jessica!" he shouts.

"At least they don't drug me to keep me compliant," she says as she takes a step toward him. "Is that what you did, Papa? I've seen the reports. Is that why I was always so tired in your huge mansion? Because you were drugging me?"

"I gave you something to help you. You were hysterical," he snarls, his mask slipping momentarily before he smiles at her again. "Everything I do is for you, printsessa. But you betray me by lying with these dogs. These men who were willing to sell you to the highest bidder. They know who you really are, Jessica, and why you are so valuable to me."

"And who is that?"

"My daughter. Your mother's daughter."

"My parents are dead," she snaps. "So, who the hell are you?"

He steps closer to her with a cruel grin on his face and I suck in a breath as my fingers squeeze the handle of my gun. Just give me a reason to shoot you in the head right now, Alexei!

"I am your father! I have been looking for you for twenty-six years!" he snarls. "They stole you from me. My own brother. It wasn't enough that he took my wife. He had to take you too. And they poisoned you against me. But you belong to me, Jessica."

"You paid the Wolf to kill my family?"

"I paid him to return what was mine."

"But my brothers? They were just children," she says. I hear the crack in her voice and wonder how much longer she's going to be able to distract him for. Glancing up to where Mikey and Liam are, I give them a subtle nod.

"Their existence was an insult to me," Alexei spits.

She moves quickly, pulling the gun from the waistband of her jeans and pressing it against his forehead, and it's clear this isn't the first time she's handled a gun like that. An unexpected surge of anger wells up in my chest as I'm forced to think about the life that Jessie has lived. Always running. Never being able to trust anyone. One of Alexei's men runs toward him, but Liam takes him out with a clean shot through the neck.

"Tell me why I shouldn't kill you right now?" she says, the tremor in her voice clearly audible.

"Because, whether or not you approve of my methods, I am your father, Jessica. One does not simply shoot their own father in the head. It is a burden I would not wish on my greatest enemy."

I step out from behind the bar. She's not going to kill him. She doesn't have it in her right now. I'm aware how much it hurts to hate your father so much you want him dead, but be unable to pull that trigger yourself.

Another of Alexei's men moves toward him and Liam takes him out too. I sense the tension in my own men creeping around the room and I hold up my hand to signal they should keep their weapons low. Not until Jessie is safe. I step closer to her, but I hold my hands up in surrender as Alexei's men eye me suspiciously.

"I hate you," Jessie says to him as the tears run down her face.

"Regardless, you are my daughter. You belong to me. I will never stop looking for you. I will never rest until you are at my side where you should have been all along."

"Never!" she hisses.

"Then you should shoot me." He looks her in the eyes and her hands tremble as she squeezes the handle but she doesn't pull the trigger.

"Jessie," I say as I approach. "Put the gun down. You don't have to do this right now."

"I do have to, Shane. Because he will never let me go. And you will always be in danger if I stay here."

"Come here and give me the gun." I hold out my hand to her before I turn to her father. "There is a rifle aimed at your head right now, Alexei. Make a move and you are dead. Do you hear that?" I shout the last part to his men. "Any shots are fired and your boss is dead."

Jessie lowers her weapon and walks backwards toward me until she is in my arms. I want to hold on tight to her and never let her go again. I want to savor the sensation of her body pressed against mine. There is so much I need to say to her. But I have to get her out of here. I press my lips against her ear. "You remember that freedom I offered you, sweetheart? The one you told me to stick up my ass?"

"Yes," she breathes.

"It's still waiting for you. The keys are where we left them. All you have to do is run."

"What about you, and Conor and the twins?" she sniffs.

"It will never be the same after all this," I tell her, even though it damn near kills me to do it. But this is the only way I see out of this right now. Alexei will never stop looking for her, and if she's here, he knows exactly where to find her. "You're not one of us. But you're not one of them either. Run, little hacker. Take your freedom. You deserve it more than anyone. Now go."

She turns to me and plants a soft kiss on my cheek. Then we

both look up at Conor and she hesitates. I know this will be breaking his heart, but I also know that he trusts me. He nods his head, and that's all the permission she needs. She runs out of the nightclub and toward the silver SUV in the garage, and straight out of our lives.

I don't have time to watch her go as Alexei shouts to his men to go after her. But they're not quick enough for Liam's sniper rifle and none of them make it anywhere near her. Alexei realizes he is not going to win this particular battle, and he uses two of his men as human shields as he makes a run for the nearest exit. I drop one of them, and Liam takes the other one out just as they reach the door, but Alexei makes it out unscathed while the rest of his men scramble for the side door.

Fuck! Another day, Alexei.

THREE OF OUR men were injured in the shoot-out, but fortunately none were killed. The same can't be said for the Russians and I have seven dead ones stinking up my club. Conor calls the clean-up crew to come deal with them while I debrief our own soldiers.

When we are are the only people left in the club , Conor walks over to Liam, Mikey and me.

"She would never have killed him. It was the only way I could buy us all some time," I say as their faces search mine for answers.

"So, that car does have a tracker, right?" Conor asks.

I raise an eyebrow at him. Does he think I'm an amateur? "Of course it does."

He nods and lets out a long, slow breath. "Thank fuck for that."

CHAPTER 16

JESSIE

TWO MONTHS LATER

a bead of sweat trickles down my back and I blow a stray strand of hair from my face as I ring up the cash register. The Arizona heat is stifling, and the air con broke a week ago. My boss, Ray, is far too cheap to have it fixed by a professional and is intent on doing it himself as soon as the part arrives. From the time it's taking, I'm pretty sure it's coming from Outer Mongolia.

Asshole!

I pick up the bottle of Jack to put it back on the shelf and it almost slips from my hands when I hear that rich, velvety voice.

"You're a hard woman to find, Jessie."

My legs tremble as I stand rooted to the spot. I place the bottle on the counter as a shudder runs down the length of my spine. If I don't turn around, maybe he won't really be here. I glance sideways at the exits, wondering if I can make a run for it.

"Oh, please go for it, Angel," he chuckles softly. "Because you know I'll catch you. And when I do, I'll enjoy nothing more than throwing you over my shoulder and carrying you to my car."

I spin around and my heart almost stops at the sight of him. He looks even better than I remember — if that were possible. In a flannel shirt, open at the collar and rolled-up sleeves that show off his muscular forearms. "I think you'll find that's kidnapping," I scowl at him.

"Well, you seemed to enjoy it the first time I kidnapped you," he winks at me. "What the hell have you done to your hair?"

I flick the ends of my now shoulder-length, brunette hair and shrug. "I fancied a change."

"I prefer it red. And long." He flashes his eyebrows at me and I have a vision of the way he used to wrap it around his fist to make me more compliant and experience a familiar fluttering between my thighs.

I fold my arms across my chest and notice his eyes drop to my cleavage as he unapologetically licks his lips. "What are you doing here, Conor?" I say with a sigh.

"I've come to bring you home."

I grind out a laugh. "I am home."

"I'm talking about your real home, Angel."

"You mean your home?"

He frowns. "Where else?"

"I think you and your brothers made it pretty clear that it wasn't my home the last time you kidnapped me!"

His Adam's apple bobs as he swallows hard. "We thought you'd betrayed us, Jessie. Just like you assumed we'd betrayed you."

"Exactly. There is no trust left between us. So, it seems the best thing to do is for all of us to go on doing our separate thing. Living our separate lives. So, please leave!"

He places those fine arms on the bar and looks around the place. There is no doubt it's seen much better days, could do with a lick of paint, some new furniture — not to mention some air-con, but it's the only bar for miles, so it's busy every night. "You can't seriously be happy here?" he asks with a tilt of his head.

"Why?" I scowl at him. "Not everyone needs five million dollar apartments and fancy sports cars to be happy."

He frowns at me. "I know that. I meant that this place doesn't exactly suit your talents, does it?"

"You have no idea what my talents are," I snap.

A wicked grin spreads across his face. "Actually, I remember exactly what your talents are, Angel. The memories keep me warm at night."

Heat sears between my thighs and I have to remind my treacherous body that we hate Conor Ryan and his brothers. "How the hell did you find me?" I say, trying to change the subject.

"With great difficulty," he grinds out the words as though it pains him to say them.

"Well, I obviously didn't do a good enough job of covering my tracks."

"Are you fucking kidding me?" he growls. "I left less than two hours after you did, and it's taken me two months to find you."

I suck in a deep breath, momentarily winded by his revelation. I had assumed they were all happy to see the back of me. I'm not one of them — that was what Shane said. "You came straight after me?" I whisper.

"Of course I did. That was always the plan. I told you that I would burn the world down to find you, Jessie. Didn't you believe me?"

"Ryan?" a voice hollers from the other side of the bar and both Conor and I glance over at my boss, Ray. "If you ain't gonna serve the guy, then I got plenty of work to keep you busy!"

I roll my eyes and turn back to Conor.

"Ryan?" he narrows those chocolate brown eyes at me and my insides melt like butter that's been left out in the Arizona heat.

"Hiding in plain sight," I say with a shrug as the heat flushes over my chest. Damn! What the hell had I been thinking choosing that name as my new identity. "Anyway," I go on before he can press me further, but there is a grin on his face that I just know is going to take some time to fade. "As you can

TWO MONTHS LATER

see, I'm working here. So, either order a drink, or be on your way."

"You got any good whiskey?"

"Plenty. But we got no Jameson's," I say, aware that's his favorite. "We have nothing Irish in this whole bar. Not until you rolled in. And I like it that way."

"You're here." He licks his lips again and a memory of him doing magical things to me with that tongue flashes into the forefront of my brain before making a direct path straight to my pussy.

"I'm not Irish. Not even a little bit. I have Russian parents and I was born and raised right here in the USA." I arch an eyebrow at him.

He leans across the bar and instinct makes me lean toward him. I regret it immediately when I realize how damn incredible he smells. "You've had so much Irish in you, I'm surprised you're not talking Gaelic," he says in a low rumble that vibrates through my whole body.

I draw in a sharp breath as a rush of heat sears between my thighs. Jesus! If I wasn't hot enough before. My panties are going to melt if I stand here talking to him much longer. "Drink?" is all I can trust myself to say.

"If you've got no Jameson's, I'll take a glass of your finest Scotch," he grins as he sits back.

I pour him a glass of the cheapest Scotch we have and place it on the bar in front of him. He takes a hundred-dollar bill out of his pocket and places it down on the bar. "Keep the change, Angel."

I roll my eyes and take his money and pocket his change. Well, a girl has to eat.

"What time does your shift end?" he says as he takes a sip of the cheap whisky and winces.

"None of your business."

"I'll just hang around until you're done, then. So, why don't

74

you fetch me a glass of that twelve year single malt you have up there?" He glances up at the top shelf.

"Oh, I can't serve you that." I shake my head.

"Why not?" he frowns.

"That's reserved for people I actually like." I sling the bar towel over my shoulder and flash him my biggest smile before I sashay down to the other end of the bar to serve another customer. I can almost feel his eyes burning into my ass and I'm so glad I wore my denim mini today.

CHAPTER 17

CONOR

*R*ay's place sure gets crowded for a run-down dive bar in the middle of nowhere. I sit on the bar stool sipping soda, my eyes never leaving Jessie. I swear every time she walks past me, she gives that sexy ass of hers an extra wiggle. The mini skirt she's wearing shows off her incredible tanned legs to perfection and her shirt has enough buttons open to give me a great view of her amazing tits too. Unfortunately, every other guy in this bar has the exact same view and that makes me pissed as hell. I've been sitting here for four hours watching her and I've had a hard on for three of those.

Each time I watch some asshole coming on to her, or drooling over her hot body, I want to jump off my stool and punch his teeth down his throat. But she handles them all with her irresistible charm and a disarming smile and none of them actually get close to laying a hand on her. I'm almost disappointed by the fact because I'd like nothing more than to take some of my frustrations out on any poor fucker who succeeded.

It has been so long since I've seen her and now that she is standing right in front of me, it is damn near killing me to sit here and keep my hands off her.

I close my eyes as she walks past me again, not even making eye contact, but I smell her as she passes me. Vanilla and cherries. My cock twitches at the memories that force themselves into my head. My head buried between her thighs. My cock buried in her hot, sweet pussy. My mouth waters as I remember how good she tastes. I would love nothing better than to lift her onto this bar, tear off her panties and eat her out right here in front of all these jackasses who assume they have a shot with her. I'd love to make them all watch her come with my mouth on her, knowing that they will never get even a chance to touch or taste her.

The other server, Cody, walks toward me and opens his mouth as if to ask me if I want a drink. I scowl at him and he scurries back along the bar, whispering something in Jessie's ear as he reaches her. His face is so close to hers, he must be able to smell her. His lips graze her hair and my hands clench into fists by my sides. She glances over at me and even from here I can see her roll her eyes before she saunters over to me.

"You going to order another drink, big guy?" she asks with a smile. "Because I got plenty of customers who would like to sit at this bar."

"Sure. I'll have another soda," I say as I place my half full glass on the bar.

"Soda?" she raises one eyebrow at me. "You sure you don't want nothing a little stronger?"

"Nope," I shake my head. "Your whisky tastes like rats' piss, and besides, I'm driving later. You don't want me driving you home drunk, do you Angel?"

She leans across the bar, and I get a perfect view of her perfect cleavage. "You won't be driving me home," she says with a smile. "I'd rather go home with any man in this bar before I let you drive me anywhere, Conor Ryan," she breathes.

"Is that so?" I narrow my eyes at her, trying to determine if she is being serious or not. I lean closer to her, standing on the edge of my stool and resting my arms on the bar. I'm so close that

I feel her breath on my cheek and the hairs on my forearms stand on end. "I'd like to see you try, Angel," I growl. "You walk out of this bar with any man but me, and I'll make sure they are the last steps he ever takes."

I hear her breath catch in her throat and she pulls back from me. There is a fire in her eyes and the skin on her neck is flushed pink, and I suppress a smile because I recognize from experience that's a sign of her being just as hot for me as I am for her. I bet if I slipped my hand beneath her skirt and inside her panties, she'd be dripping wet for me. My hot, horny angel.

Two hours after she left our club in New York, I was on her tail, but she had dumped the SUV and was in the wind and I've been looking for her ever since. There were times when I worried I would never find her, and the prospect of living the rest of my life without her made me feel like I might fucking die. But, then I ended up here, in this tiny town in the asshole of Arizona, and there she was.

Even though she's changed her hair, I recognized her immediately. I sat in my car, in a spot just fifty yards up the road from her apartment, and watched her walk out of the door before climbing into a beat-up green Mustang. My heart almost stopped beating in my chest and I couldn't even move. I just sat and watched her and let the sight of her flood my senses until it felt like I was finally alive for the first time since she'd left.

An hour later, when I got here to Ray's bar, I wanted to pull her into my arms and never let her go. Kiss her smart mouth until she agreed to come home with me. I still do. But that is not the Jessie I know and love. She would never make it that easy on me.

"A soda then?" she says as she blows a stray strand of hair from her eyes.

"Please," I reply with a smile.

"Coming right up."

CHAPTER 18

JESSIE

*C*onor sits at the end of the bar for the remainder of my shift. The place has been packed for the last five hours of it, and I've barely had a chance to speak to him, which is only a good thing. I tried to get my work buddy, Cody, to serve him, but he flat out refused. I suspect the fact that Conor spent most of the night glaring at him, especially when we had to squeeze past each other behind the narrow bar, kind of put him off. So, I have been serving him soda all night, most of which he's left to go warm in this intense heat.

When there is no-one left but him, I walk over to him. "We're closing up. You need to leave."

"Let me give you a ride?" he offers.

"I have a car."

"I have a better one," he grins.

"Probably. But mine has one huge advantage."

"And what's that?" he smirks.

"You won't be in it."

"Ouch!" he says as he places his hand over his heart. "I'll be waiting outside anyway, Angel. In case you change your mind."

"I won't," I snap as he stands up and walks out of the bar.

Ten minutes later, I'm walking through the parking lot. Conor's huge Audi SUV is parked next to my old, beat-up Mustang and he's leaning against my car with his arms folded.

"Can you move, please?" I snipe.

"Sure, Angel." He steps aside, and I eye him warily as I open my car and climb inside. He stands watching me as I start it up.

My car is old, but it's a beast and I love the roar of the engine when it fires up. Tonight, though, it sputters and dies. I roll down the window. "What the hell did you do to my car?"

He opens his mouth and feigns his indignation. "Me? Nothing," he smirks. "Do you need a ride?"

I get out and slam the door. Cody has left. Ray has gone too, and I'm so desperate that I would even consider getting a ride home with my handsy, jackass of a boss. We are in the middle of nowhere and my place is at least an hour's walk away and Conor Ryan is looking like my only option.

"This means nothing, Conor," I snap as I walk toward his car. "You can drop me at home and then hightail your ass back to New York."

"Whatever you say, Angel."

WE DRIVE in silence and I realize that I haven't given Conor my address, but he's heading straight to it.

"We could just stay on the road and head home to New York right now?" he says as he turns to me.

"Are you serious?" I scowl at him.

"Deadly."

"You honestly think I would just pack up and leave my whole life here to come back to New York with you? What planet are you living on, Conor?"

"What have you got here that's so important to you, Jessie, or Ryan, is it now? Are you seeing someone?" he growls.

"No!" I snap. "Not that it's any of your business. And what I have here is my life, Conor. It might not seem like much to you, but it is freedom. It's paying bills, and grocery shopping, and going to work. It is life!"

I sit back in my seat and fold my arms across my chest, and he falls silent. A short time later, we pull up outside my apartment.

"Thanks." I snap as I go to open the door, but he locks it with the push of a button, and my heart lurches in my chest. "Let me out," I demand.

"Jessie. Can we just talk? Please?"

"I have nothing to say to you. Now, let me out of this car or, I swear to God, I will kick out the windshield."

He sighs and the next thing I hear is the doors unlocking with a click. My fingers curl around the handle, but something stops me opening it immediately.

"What time shall I pick you up for your shift tomorrow?" he asks.

"What?" I blink.

"You have no car. Remember?"

"I'll get a ride off Cody."

"That stoner you work with? I don't think so, Angel," he scowls at me. "I'll just sit out here all night if I have to."

I stare at him. I wouldn't put it past him to do just that. "Fine. My shift starts at eleven."

"I'll be here at ten then."

I sit looking at him and there is a gigantic ball of emotion in my chest that I can't deal with. I have thought about him and his brothers every day since I left, and seeing him sitting right here in front of me makes me realize how much I have missed them all.

What happens next happens entirely on instinct. I lunge for him, wrapping my hands around his neck and pulling his face to mine. He unclips his seatbelt and reaches over to me, lifting me with ease and pulling me onto his lap so I'm straddling him. His hard cock presses against me through my damp panties as my skirt rides up my thighs, causing pleasure to flood my entire body.

My heart hammers against my chest as his fingers dig into my hips and he pulls me closer, grinding his cock against my pussy and making me moan softly. I press my mouth over his and he licks the seam of my lips until I open them and allow his tongue inside. The warmth in my core spreads through my chest and my limbs as I melt into his fierce kiss.

I press my breasts against his muscular chest and my nipples stiffen until they're almost painful. My hands run over his muscular shoulders and they flex beneath his shirt, reminding me exactly how ripped his body is.

"Jessie," he groans into my mouth, and his voice rumbles through my body. His hands slide down to my ass and he squeezes me exactly the way I like it until the memories of all the incredible times we have spent together flood my senses. I feel an intense rush of slick heat between my thighs as he fucks my mouth with his tongue. Damn! I'm about to reach the point of no return here. If we don't stop now, I'm going to ride him like a rodeo bull right here in his car.

It takes every ounce of willpower I have, but I pull back from him and wipe my mouth with my thumb and index finger. "Night, big guy," I pant.

"Jessie," he growls. "Let me come up to your place with you. Let me take you to bed, Angel. I need you so fucking bad."

I need him too. But I can't do this. "No. We can't," I shake my head.

"Then what the hell was that?" he blinks at me.

"That was goodbye. Go home, Conor," I say. Pain flickers over his face and I force myself to close my eyes because I can't stand to see it as I climb off his lap and out of his car. I walk toward my apartment with tears running down my cheeks. But this is for the best.

CHAPTER 19

CONOR

*L*ooking out of the window at Jessie's incredible ass in that tiny mini skirt, sashaying up the steps to her apartment, has my cock weeping for her. What would she do if I jumped out of this car and ran up those steps after her? Pushed her against her front door and fucked her right up against it? Because that's what I want to do more than anything and it's taking every single ounce of restraint I have not to.

I press the call button on the steering wheel of my car and call Shane. He answers on the third ring. "Hey, Con. Any news?"

"Yeah. I found her, bro."

He sighs deeply. "Where is she?"

"Arizona. Working in some dive bar."

"A bar?"

"Yup. I had to sit and watch all night while a bunch of drunk assholes were hitting on our girl. I was praying that one of them would touch her, just to give me a chance to break some faces."

He laughs softly. "I take it no-one touched her then?"

"No. She's still the same fiery little pocket rocket who left us two months ago. They wouldn't dare," I laugh too.

There are a few seconds' silence before Shane speaks again. "Is she with you?"

"No. She told me to go to hell, but, I'm working on her. I'm picking her up for her shift tomorrow."

"Be careful she doesn't run," he warns. "I need you back here."

"I know. But she has no wheels right now. I took the coil cable out of her car for her."

"You think you can bring her back?"

"I sure as hell ain't leaving here without her."

"Hmm," he mumbles, and I sense he's distracted.

"How are you getting on your end?" I lean back in my seat and glance up at Jessie's window.

"Still no sign of Alexei. He's gone underground. Did Jessie mention if she knows where he is?"

"We didn't make it that far, bro. She wasn't exactly pleased to see me."

"I guess not. I've been looking into the Wolf again too. Jessie is convinced he's still alive and maybe he can give us some answers."

"Any luck?"

"None at all," he sighs and then he's quiet again.

"Something else going on, Shane?" I frown.

A few seconds pass before he answers. "He's sick."

It takes me a second to register who he's talking about and bile surges from my stomach, burning against the back of my throat as soon as I do. I swallow it down. "How sick?"

"Very. Lung cancer. It's terminal."

"Good. I hope he dies a very slow and very fucking painful death. I hope that cunt lives every second of the rest of his miserable life in excruciating pain. I hope he dies in a pool of his own vomit and piss. But, most of all, I pray that he dies alone, crying for someone to help him. Just like she did."

"Yeah, me too," he replies softly.

"When did you find out?" I snarl as adrenaline starts to thunder around my body.

"Yesterday. Erin told me."

"Figures she'd know," I snap. Erin is our family lawyer, and Shane's ex-fiancée. She moved to New York from Ireland at the same time as we did, and she has the unfortunate role of being the conduit between my father and Shane. None of us have spoken directly to him since we left Ireland ten years ago, but Shane communicates with him via Erin when he absolutely has to. Shane was our father's pride and joy. His first born son — he would have been his only son if my cunt of a father would have had his way.

"Are you visiting him?" I ask.

"Of course not, Con. What the fuck?"

I wince, feeling guilty for even asking that. The truth is, Shane probably hates our father even more than me and the twins do.

"But when he dies, I will have to go to Ireland and sort out his estate," he says with a sigh.

"I know. Have you told Mikey and Liam?"

"Yeah."

"They okay?"

"They need you back here. They need Jessie back too."

"And what about you?" I ask him. He will never admit that he needs her just as much as we do, even though it's completely obvious.

"Just get your asses home as soon as you can. I don't care if you have to tie her up and put her in the trunk."

"Yeah, well, that's kind of my plan B," I only half joke, because if Jessie doesn't agree to come with me of her own free will, I don't know what I'll do, and I am not averse to kidnapping her for a third time.

"Erin's here. I have to go. Keep me posted."

"Will do. Bye, bro," I say before I end the call. I lean back against the headrest and suck in a lungful of air as I try and suppress the memories of my childhood and teenage years that any mention of my father dredges up. I hate that vile piece of shit more than anyone in this world. The fact that he is dying should bring me some comfort, or some peace, but it doesn't.

I look up at the door to Jessie's apartment again and unclip my seatbelt. I want her so fucking bad, I feel like I can't breathe without her. My fingers grip the door handle and my heart races in my chest. What if she tells me to go when I need her to want me to stay so much?

The light in her apartment goes out and I sit back in my seat again and let out a long breath. I'll have to wait until tomorrow.

CHAPTER 20

JESSIE

*W*alking through my apartment, I throw my purse straight onto the sofa and head to my bedroom. I should be exhausted. I usually am after a ten-hour shift, but my mind is racing and my body is sizzling with energy. As I lick my lips, I can still taste him on me and it makes the heat sear between my thighs.

I turn on the lamp on my nightstand and lie on my bed, taking deep breaths to calm my racing heart. I'd convinced myself that I'd never see any of the Ryan brothers ever again. And I made sure I covered my tracks well, or at least I thought I had. Maybe, subconsciously, I left a single breadcrumb for them to find.

Whatever it was, Conor has found me and I would bet my ass he is still sitting outside in his expensive car, watching, waiting to see if I'm going to run.

I'm tempted to go to the window and look out, but I daren't, because if I see him out there, looking up at this window, I might just run out of this apartment, jump back into his car and ask him to take me home.

As if I've been living in a dream world these past two months, the reality of my whole life suddenly hits me. Who was I kidding, thinking I could disappear from the face of the earth and live anything like a regular life? That's not who I am.

I'll admit it's been kind of nice pretending to be completely normal for a while. But I'm not normal. I'm Jessica Romanov and I've been seeking revenge on the men responsible for slaughtering my family for the past ten years. And now I have an opportunity to exact my revenge on one of them, at least: Alexei Ivanov - the man who claims to be my biological father.

Whether he is or not, he killed my family. My beautiful, kind mom. The only father I have ever known, a man I respected and adored and who taught me everything I know, and my adorable little brothers. And not content with taking that family from me, he took the only other family I have ever felt a part of too, when he found me in New York and filled my head with lies. For a short while, I was Jessie Ryan, and I was as happy as I'd ever been in my life.

Alexei took it all from me and I won't rest until he takes his dying breath. I told Conor that I'm not going back to New York with him and I wasn't exactly lying when I said that. I'm still fooling myself that I can stay here a little longer and be Ryan, the brunette from the bar who can do five shots of whisky in a row and still dance the Chattahoochee, instead of Jessie, the red-headed hacker whose father is the psychopathic head of the Bratva.

Reaching over, I turn off the lamp. If Conor is outside watching, maybe that will make him leave, and I won't have to think about him sitting out there alone in his car. I hope it will deter him from coming up here and knocking on my door, because if he does, I don't think I have the strength to turn him away.

My body aches for him. I had closed that part of myself off, and less than an hour alone in his company and I'm burning up with longing and dripping wet for him. Damn those Ryan brothers and their fine asses.

I pull up my skirt and slip my hand inside my panties,

spreading my legs wide as I circle two fingers over my swollen clit. My fingers glide easily over the slick bud of flesh. Closing my eyes, I imagine that it's Conor's fingers on me instead of my own. My orgasm builds quickly until I'm pushing my hips up to meet my hand. Using my other hand, I slide two fingers inside myself and the rush of warm wetness pools there. I recall the taste of Conor's lips. His tongue in my mouth. How good his tongue feels on my pussy. How incredible he smells and how hard he fucks me. I move my fingers faster as I picture his face and pretend that he is in here with me, watching me come for him and waiting to claim me for his own.

When my climax tears through me a few moments later, I bite down on my lip to stop myself from crying out his name, even though I know he won't hear me. I lie back against my pillow, breathless and wanting. Instead of relieving any tension, getting myself off has only made me want him more.

I need to remind myself that I came this far on my own. I don't need Conor or his brothers. I don't want any of it anymore. I am building a new life for myself, and the Ryans can't be any part of it.

CHAPTER 21

JESSIE

*T*he following morning, I check outside as soon as I wake up and I'm both relieved and disappointed to find that Conor's car is not outside. I eat breakfast and make some coffee and wonder if he left for New York or whether he's still hanging around nearby. And if he has left, how the hell am I going to get to work today? I can't even ask Cody for a ride as he's on a late shift and he'll sleep until at least noon. I should probably call a cab.

As I head to the bedroom to look for my cell phone, a knock at my front door stops me in my tracks.

I freeze. I never have visitors to my place, so this can only be one person. Turning on my heel, I walk over to answer it and see the unmistakable figure of Conor through the glass. Despite everything I said last night, my stomach flutters in excitement.

Opening the door, I am confronted by his six foot two frame dressed in jeans and a tightly fitted shirt, looking good enough to lick from head to toe. "I thought you were going home?"

He leans against my doorframe, his legs crossed at the ankle and his arms crossed over his chest. "I've been looking for you every minute of every day for two months, Jessie. I'm not going home until you agree to come with me."

"Well, you'd better get used to this Arizona heat, big guy," I smile.

He narrows his eyes at me. "You ready?"

"Sure," I shrug, grabbing my purse from the table and closing the door behind me. "I hope you're going to pay for my car to get fixed?" I say as we walk across the road to his car.

"Why would I do that?" he grins at me. "I had nothing to do with that old rust-bucket refusing to start last night."

"She is not a rust-bucket!" I snap. "And yes you did!"

He shakes his head and unlocks the doors, allowing us both to climb inside. Once we're buckled up, he pulls away from the curbside and I turn the radio to a country music station, because I'm aware he hates it, but he doesn't change it back. I sing along — badly — as we drive along the highway.

The air con is on full, but despite that, a bead of sweat trickles down my spine. Being so close to him, confined in such a small space, is maddening. I glance sideways at him and remember how I almost jumped his bones last night. How good it felt to have his hard cock rubbing against my pussy as I straddled him. He clears his throat and I wonder if he's thinking about it too. I glance down at his huge thighs encased in his jeans, almost busting out of the denim as his muscles stretch the fabric taut. Damn! No man has any right to be so freaking fine!

He shifts gear and his knuckles brush the skin of my outer thigh as he does, making my breath catch in my throat and goose-bumps prickle along my arms. He keeps his hand on the shift stick and I edge a tiny bit closer to the center console, as discreetly as I can. All the while I look down at his huge powerful forearm and that sexy Breitling watch he wears, and recall all the times I have held on to that arm while he finger fucked me. The thought sends a rush of wet heat flushing between my thighs. I swallow hard and turn my head to the window. I need to get out of this car before I ask him to pull over and fuck me in the back seat.

"I've missed you, Angel," he says softly, and I turn my head back to him.

"Don't, Conor," I say with a sigh.

"Why?" he frowns at me before turning back to the road.

I want to tell him that it doesn't matter if he missed me because he means nothing to me anymore. But I can't because I promised him I would never lie to him again and that would be the biggest whopper in the history of untruths. "Because it doesn't change anything," I say instead.

"Did you miss me?"

I turn back to the window and don't answer. If I admit that I missed him, then it's only a matter of time before something more happens between us. The tension in the car is so obvious I feel like I can actually see it. The air sizzles with electricity and desire. I'm hyper aware of everything. Our breathing and the way it's steadily gotten heavier in the past few minutes. I can even hear him licking his lip and I can't stop the memory of him running his tongue all over my body from overwhelming me. I close my eyes and will him to let this go.

"Jessie!" he snaps and I draw in a deep breath before I turn back to him.

"You know I did, Conor. But things are different now."

His hand still rests on the shift-stick and he reaches out his finger and strokes it gently across the edge of my knee, sending tiny sparks of electricity shooting straight up my thigh and making me visibly shiver in my seat. "Not everything though?" he growls, and the sound vibrates through my body until it rolls through my abdomen and straight to my pussy.

"No. Not everything," I breathe and the corners of his mouth pull into a smile before we drive the rest of the way in silence.

· · ·

CONOR INSISTS on helping me to open up once we get to Ray's bar, and I can't decide whether I'm annoyed or delighted by this.

"Are you here on your own?" he frowns at me once we're inside.

"Yeah. Ray will be here at one. We hardly get any customers before then, anyway. And we had a delivery this morning. Ray comes in to take it in but he won't put it away on account of his bad back," I say with a roll of my eyes.

"So he leaves it all for you to put away?" he frowns at the huge stack of boxes near the basement door.

"I'm perfectly capable of hauling some boxes down to the basement."

"I know. But that doesn't mean he should just leave it all for you."

"Well, it's kind of my job." I arch an eyebrow at him as I walk to the basement and open the door, propping it ajar with one of the boxes.

Conor puts his keys and his cell on the bar and walks over to me. "Let me help."

"I'm fine," I snap.

"For fuck's sake, Jessie!" he snaps back.

I stand and stare at him with my hands on my hips. His help would let me get the job done in less than half the time. "Fine. Start with that pile over there," I point to the stack of Bud Light near the jukebox.

I walk down the basement stairs with the first box before leaving it at the bottom. I'm about to head up for the next one when Conor walks down, carrying two at once. Show-off!

"You stay down here and put them away and I'll bring them down to you?" he suggests.

"Fine," I roll my eyes. "But once we've finished this, you need to leave. Ray won't be happy if he finds out you're distracting me."

"You think I give a shit what Ray thinks?" he says as he walks up the steps.

"I know that you don't, but I do, Conor. This is my job, and as much as Ray is an asshole, I kind of like it here. So, I need you to leave before he gets in."

He turns and stops at the top of the stairs. "Dammit, Jessie!" he scowls at me as he bends to pick up a box. "Can you please just-"

"Conor! Don't ..." I shout, but he's already headed back down the steps and the door is closing behind him. It slams shut with a loud bang, plunging the basement into darkness.

"Shit!" I hiss as I hear Conor's footsteps reaching the bottom. He puts the box down by my feet and breathes heavily near my ear.

"Where is the light?" he whispers.

"There isn't one!"

"What? Why?" Panic makes his voice crack.

"Because it shorted a week ago along with the air-con and Ray is too cheap to get someone in to fix it."

"What the fuck? Then let's get out of here." He turns, as if to walk back up the steps but he doesn't move.

"The door doesn't open from the inside," I sigh.

"What?" he breathes and I hear the panic setting into his voice. "That's fucking illegal or something. It's a fire hazard."

"Yeah? Well, Ray's not really big on health and safety. That's why I had the box holding open the door, asshole." I nudge him in the ribs, or at least I assume it's his ribs, because I can't see a thing.

"Jessie! We can't stay in here. There must be a way out," he says and the fear in his voice is clearly audible now, as well as the labored sound of his breathing, which grows heavier and faster with each passing second.

Shit! I forgot he's claustrophobic. He hates the dark or confined spaces. He has done ever since he was kidnapped by the

Russians almost two years ago and they kept him locked up in a basement.

"Hey," I reach out, searching for his face and place my hand on his cheek. "Ray will be here in an hour or so. This room is huge. There's plenty of air down here. We're going to be fine."

"We need to get the fuck out of here," he snarls as he runs up the steps and pushes against the door. Then I hear him trying to kick it open as his breathing becomes increasingly labored.

"Conor. That's a fire door. It's not going to open. Please come back down here and sit with me."

He ignores me and continues pummeling the door. "Conor!" I shout and he stops. The sound of his footsteps signal him coming back down the wooden stairs. I reach for him as soon as I sense him close to me. Running my hands over his chest, his heart hammers beneath my fingertips as his breathing grows faster and heavier. My own heart races too, but for an entirely different reason.

"Conor. Listen to me. We're going to be fine. Ray will be here soon. Or a customer will come in. And then we can shout for help. Okay?" I say as softly and calmly as I can.

"What if no-one comes?" he gasps for breath.

Shit! He's about to have a panic attack. "Someone will come. I won't let anything happen to you. I promise," I say as I slide my hands up to his face. I lean up onto my tiptoes and press my lips softly against his. "We'll be okay," I whisper as I keep peppering butterfly kisses over his lips and jaw. I need to distract him and this is the surest way I know how.

He wraps his arms around my waist, and I press my body close to his. Electricity crackles between us. His heart is still pounding, but his breathing is becoming less erratic. I seal my mouth over his and kiss him softly as my hands move up to his hair and I tug it gently, just the way he likes it, making him groan softly.

I slide one hand to the back of his neck and press his face

closer to mine. He seems hesitant at first, still panicking about being trapped in this room. As I slide my tongue into his mouth, I feel the change in him and the growl in his throat vibrates through his whole chest. His hands drop to my ass and he slips his tongue against mine as he walks me backwards. We stumble in the darkness until we come up against the cold concrete wall and as our bodies press together, heat floods my core.

I wrap my arms around his neck and pull him closer to me as he pushes his hard body against mine, pinning me to the wall as he deepens our kiss. I claw at his neck. His kisses are always full of fire and passion, but this is like a raging inferno between us. He devours my mouth like he might never get the chance to taste me again and I melt into him, taking every single thing he has to give as he claims me for his own once more.

Every nerve ending in my body comes alive with electricity and fire as wet heat sears between my thighs and my body sizzles with the need for him. I reach for his belt, tugging it open before I unzip his fly. Sliding my hand into his jeans, I take hold of his hot, stiff cock and squeeze him.

"Jessie," he groans. "Don't start something you can't finish. Because I need to feel you so bad, Angel, and I won't be able to stop if we go any further."

"I need you too, Conor," I breathe as my heartbeat starts to pound in my ears. "I want to feel you inside me. There's been no-one else," I assure him, because we have no condoms down here, and I hope that he can say the same.

"Good, because I'd have no choice but to kill anyone who put his hands on you," he growls as his hands slide to my sides and he lifts my denim mini up over my hips until it's bunched around my waist. Then his hand slips between my thighs, and my legs almost buckle as he roughly tugs my panties to the side and slides two fingers through my folds. The warmth floods my core and I experience an intense rush of wetness. I push my hips against his hand and moan loudly. My body remembers his touch so well, and every part of me aches for him. My pussy throbs with need as he glides over my entrance.

"Please, Conor!" I beg and he smiles against my skin.

"I've missed this hot, wet pussy, Angel," he breathes as he slides two fingers deep inside me and the rush of slick heat almost makes me pass out. I cling to him and whimper shamelessly as he fucks me with his skilled fingers. He reaches deep inside, curling the tip of them against my G-spot and causing tremors to vibrate through my stomach and thighs. The wet sound of my arousal echoes around the basement and it makes everything seem even hotter than it already is.

"You hear how wet you are for me, Jessie?" he growls. "I'm going to have to make you come with my fingers first because I am so fucking hard for you, I'm not going to last more than five minutes once I get my cock in you."

"God, I've missed your filthy mouth," I pant.

"You're going to get my mouth later. But I might embarrass myself if I taste your pussy right now. I haven't even jerked off this morning," he chuckles softly and my insides melt like warm butter at the sound. Not being able to see seems to heighten my other senses. Even the smell of him is driving me crazy. I had forgotten how deliciously intoxicating he was.

"Conor," I pant as my orgasm builds, pulsing through my thighs and my core. He rubs the pad of his thumb over my clit as he nuzzles my neck and my climax crashes over me like a tsunami. My walls clench around his fingers and my entire body trembles with the intensity of my release.

He sucks gently on my neck as he slides his fingers out, and then he lifts me so I can wrap my shaking legs around his waist. His cock nudges at my opening and I suck air through my teeth as the tip pushes into my wet heat.

"You want this, Angel?" he growls.

"Yes," I pant as I claw at his neck and push my hips against him.

With a roll of his hips, he pushes deep inside me and I moan so loudly that it echoes around the basement. He fills me so completely and I'm overwhelmed by the feelings of relief and euphoria that course around my body as the tears roll down my cheeks.

"I've missed you so much," I breathe as he starts to nail me against the wall. I no longer have any defenses against him and realize I was only fooling myself thinking that I had any to begin with. He owns me completely.

"Your pussy feels so fucking good, Jessie," he groans as he continues pounding me. "It was made for my cock. I am never letting you go again. Do you understand me?"

I don't answer him. I can't because I am completely lost in him.

CONOR SITS on the floor with his back to the wall and his legs outstretched. I'm curled on his lap with his huge arms wrapped around me and I smile in contentment. My hand is on his chest and his heart hammers beneath my fingertips.

"Are you okay?" I whisper.

"Better than okay, Angel."

"Your heart is still pounding."

"Yeah? But now it's fuck all to do with being stuck in this basement," he laughs softly.

"Hmm. That was pretty amazing," I smile as I snuggle closer against his chest.

"Tell me that wasn't a goodbye fuck?" he says, his lips pressed against my ear.

"Of course it wasn't."

"Come home, Jessie," he breathes against my hair.

"I can't," I whisper.

"Why?"

"Because it's not the same. I don't think I could ever feel the same living there. Not after everything that happened. Everything that's been said."

He brushes my hair back from my face and presses a kiss against my temple. "He wants you back too."

A sob catches in my throat. "He doesn't, Conor. He hates me for what I did to you all."

"No, he doesn't. Come home and talk to him."

"I'm not sure I can face him," I murmur.

"Then fuck Shane! I need you back home. Aren't I enough for you Angel?"

I press my face against his neck. "You know that you are."

"So, come back with me?"

"Stay with me?" I counter.

We're both saved from answering by the door swinging open, flooding the basement with light once more. "Ryan! What the hell is going on down there?" Ray shouts.

I stand up, brushing the dust from my skirt, and Conor jumps up beside me. "That stupid door closed on me," I shout back.

Ray peers inside and then his face wrinkles in disgust. "You think you can use my bar as a motel to screw your boyfriends?" he snarls, and Conor rushes past me, running up the stairs in two seconds flat.

"Don't you ever fucking speak to her like that," he snarls and Ray steps back as Conor advances on him. I run up the stairs and put my hand on Conor's shoulder. "Please, don't," I whisper against his ear.

"You're not getting paid for the time you've spent down there," Ray snaps.

I push past Conor and square up to my boss myself. "I have put up with you being cheap and crass and condescending for the past six weeks, because I liked this town and this job. But we were just trapped down there for over an hour because of your cheap ass ways, and I will not have you putting your shit on me, Ray. You can take your job and shove it up your fat ass!"

Conor chuckles behind me, but Ray stands there staring at me, his mouth opening and closing like a goldfish. "Okay," he holds up his hands. "I won't take it out of your pay."

"Too late," I snap as I start to make my way toward the door.

"But, Ryan. Who'll cover the lunch shift?" he wails, but I am already halfway out the door and Conor is on my heels.

I walk out into the parking lot and blink in the glare of the midday sun. I glance over at my old green Mustang with its windows that will only roll part way down, and then at Conor's shiny SUV, with working air-con and luxury leather seats.

He holds out his hand. "Come home, Angel? Everybody wants you back. They sent me to get you because we couldn't all take two months off work to find you."

I look at his outstretched hand.

"Please?" he says.

As I think about the stuff in my apartment, I realize there is nothing there that I need. My cell isn't even a smartphone. I always travel light — a few clothes and toiletries. Turning away from Conor, I walk over to my Mustang and pop the trunk.

"Jessie!" Conor shouts after me, his dark brown eyes imploring me.

I take the backpack from inside. I'm always ready to move on at a moment's notice and this bag contains everything I need for a two and a half thousand mile road trip. Hoisting it over my shoulder, I close the trunk.

Conor narrows his eyes as I walk back toward him, as if he's not quite sure whether I'm about to run. "Come on then, big guy," I say, nodding toward his car, and his handsome face breaks into a huge grin. He steps closer to me, picks me up in his arms and spins me around, making me giggle. "I love you, Jessie Ryan," he says before he seals my mouth with a kiss.

CHAPTER 22

CONOR

J look across at her as she fastens her seatbelt and smile. Leaving this dust bowl without her was never an option, but I can't describe the sheer relief I feel at having her sitting here in my car after agreeing to come back to New York.

"Shall we hit the road?" she says as she kicks off her sandals and puts her feet up on the dash, ensuring I get an incredible view of her tanned legs in her denim mini.

"Do you need to go to your place on the way?"

"No," she shakes her head. "There's nothing there I need."

"Good," I breathe a sigh of relief. Stopping by her place could have been an opportunity for her to run. "But before we set off, I need to do something." Taking my cell out of my pocket, I dial Liam's number. A few seconds later, his face fills the screen.

"You got some good news, bro?" he says when he answers.

"I sure have." I grin at him as I turn the phone so he can see my passenger.

"Jessie!" he shouts. "Please tell me you're coming home?"

I watch the blush creep across her cheeks as she smiles. "Yeah," she says with a shrug. "If you're all okay with that?"

"Okay with it? Fuck, baby, we miss you like crazy," he chuckles. I shift over in my seat so both Jessie and I can see the screen. "Mikey!" Liam shouts and a few seconds later my other younger brother's face appears on the screen too.

"Red!" he grins. "What the fuck have you done to your hair?"

"It will grow out," she says with a roll of her eyes.

"It better. So, you coming home?"

"Yes," she laughs.

"Great. Get your asses on a plane right now and we'll be waiting for you at the airport," Mikey says and Liam nods in agreement.

Jessie looks across at me, biting her lower lip in a way that makes me want to bite every part of her body, and I wink at her. "Actually, we're going to drive back," I say.

"What?" Liam groans.

"Fuck, no!" Mikey shouts.

"I can't just leave the car here—" I say.

"It's just a car. We'll have someone pick it up," Liam interrupts me.

"Jessie. You want to fly, right?" Mikey asks. "You don't want to spend three days in a car with Conor, do you?"

"Three?" I shake my head and glance sideways at Jessie, and she grins at me. "More like five?"

"Yeah. I'd say five," she nods in agreement.

"No!" the twins shout in unison. "You got to get your asses back here right now. Conor, you know what a pain in the ass Shane is when he's in a bad mood. Please don't subject us to more of his moodiness than is necessary," Mikey adds.

I sense Jessie bristle at the mention of Shane's name. I slide my hand over her thigh and squeeze gently as Mikey and Liam go on grumbling. "Boys," I shout in order to be heard over their grumbling. "Let me show you something." I tilt the phone down so they can see Jessie's gorgeous legs in her tiny skirt and my hand sliding between them. They both groan and growl in appreciation and I laugh as I lean back in my seat and turn the phone back to me. "Now, can you honestly tell me that if either of you were in my shoes, you would be doing anything but driving back to New York – very slowly?"

They both frown at me and voice their disapproval, and Jessie chuckles in her seat beside me.

"You got four days, Conor!" Liam snaps. "And then we'll be coming to get our girl ourselves."

I nod. "Deal. Now say goodbye to Jessie, and she'll call you later tonight when we stop at a motel."

As I turn the screen again, I watch while Jessie waves and blows them a kiss. "See you soon, boys."

"See you in four days," I wink at my brothers before ending the call. "You sure you're okay with driving home to New York?" I ask her as I put the car into drive.

"Four days on the road with you? Staying at cheap roadside motels every night?" she bites on her lip again as though she's deep in thought and my cock twitches at the sight. "I'm sure I can handle that."

I pull the car out of the parking lot and raise an eyebrow at her. "Hmm. But can I, Angel?"

"Well, I can't wait to find out, big guy," she smiles at me.

"Me neither."

WE HIT the road as soon as I ended the call to Liam and Mikey and I've been driving for six hours by the time we stop at a motel.

"You want me to drive us a little further?" Jessie asks.

I roll my neck, making it crack. "No. I'm beat. Besides, I need food. Man cannot survive on candy alone." I wink at her. I asked her to get some snacks when we stopped for gas earlier and she bought candy, and more candy. "Besides, by the time we've eaten, it will be late. We can set off again early in the morning."

"Okay," she climbs out of the car and takes her backpack from the back seat. "Shall we see if they have a room first?"

"Sure."

TEN MINUTES LATER, I open the door to our motel room. It's nothing fancy, but it's clean. Jessie walks inside and flops down into the middle of the large bed and my cock stirs to attention. Suddenly, I feel like a horny teenager. When we had sex in that basement earlier, it was incredible. But it was rushed and frantic. The fulfilling of a carnal need. And the thought of spending the entire night with her, naked and in that bed, makes me nervous and excited. I don't think I have ever felt like this in my whole life about the prospect of spending the night with a woman.

She looks up at me, her blue eyes dark with desire, and I have to drag my eyes away from her as my stomach growls and reminds me I need food — like now.

"Come on. Let's go eat?" I drop my bag on the carpet and hold my hand out to her.

"That place next door looks like it does takeout," she says as she stretches her legs and yawns. "I don't want to go out. Let's lay on the bed, watch TV and eat until we can't move?"

I stare at her as I consider her offer. I could go for takeout. It would probably be quicker too. "Okay." I run a hand over my jaw. "What do you fancy?"

"A big dirty burger," she grins. "And a Coke."

"Dirty burger and a Coke," I nod. "I'll be back in fifteen."

I OPEN the door with the bag of takeout in my hand, and the first thing I notice is that Jessie isn't lying on the bed. I step inside. She's not in the room.

"Jessie!" I shout as I head to the bathroom, but the door is open and I already know instinctively that she's not in there. My heart drops through my chest. The first opportunity she got, she ditched me. How the fuck does this girl keep making a fool out of me?

"Fuck!" I shout, punching the bathroom door and putting a hole right through it, just as I hear voices outside.

The door opens and Jessie is standing there with an old lady with gray hair. "Here he is. I'm sure Conor will be able to sort it for you," Jessie says as she smiles at me.

"What?" I can't help but frown as adrenaline is still thundering around my body.

"This is Barbara from down the hall. She can't get the faucet to turn on and there is no-one on the desk. I tried, but it's stuck fast. You think you can take a look?"

I take a deep breath and will my heart to stop racing. "Yeah. Course," I say walking out of the room and along the corridor behind Jessie and Barbara.

A few minutes later, I've fixed the stuck faucet and Jessie and I walk back to our room after Barbara insists that I take a packet of M&M's for my trouble. As soon as the door is closed behind us, I pull her into my arms. "Don't disappear on me like that again, Angel," I warn her.

"I'm sorry. But she knocked, and she needed help. I was only a few minutes."

"I thought you'd gone, Jessie. Or something had happened to you." I swallow the emotion that wells up into my throat.

"I'm not going anywhere, big guy," she smiles at me and I press a kiss on her forehead.

"Good. Now let's eat before I fucking pass out."

We finally sit down at the small table and Jessie takes the food out of the bag. It smells incredible and my stomach growls in agreement. We eat in silence for a few moments and I can sense the tension growing in the small room. She looks across at me and I know the question is coming.

"What happened after I left?"

"We didn't kill him," I tell her. "When you left, I don't know, maybe we got distracted. Your father–"

"He's not my father," she interrupts me.

"Alexei got out of there. Him and a few of his men."

"And the rest?"

"Dead. He basically used them as human shields. Didn't you know he was still alive?"

She shakes her head. "No. I ran here and then I haven't even opened a laptop or been online at all. I didn't even have a smartphone. I wanted to leave it all behind. I thought perhaps if I tried to be this completely different person, he would never find me."

I finish my burger and wipe my hands on a napkin. "You really didn't want anyone to find you? You'd rather have stayed in Arizona?"

"Well, I thought so. But then you showed up and I now all I can think about is how much I've left behind. And how much Alexei Ivanov has already taken from me. Not just my family, but the new family I'd found too," she says as tears form in her eyes.

I reach out and place my hand over hers. "Your new family is still right here, Angel."

"Some of you are," she sniffs.

I lean back in the chair. Shane! She worries so much about what he thinks of her, but then we all do. He is the head of the family, after all. My brothers and I can't stand to disappoint him, and it seems that Jessie feels exactly the same. I wish I could help her understand him a little more, then she would see how much she means to him. But it's something she needs to figure out on her own.

She wipes her eyes and pushes her chair back, leaving her half-eaten burger on the table. "Thanks for dinner. I'm going to grab a quick shower. I feel sticky," she says, bending to give me a kiss on the cheek.

I watch her walking away, contemplating following her in there, but I get the sense she wants to be alone.

CHAPTER 23

JESSIE

I flick through the TV channels as I lie on the bed while Conor takes a shower. He has more clothes than I do, so I'm wearing one of his t-shirts and nothing else. No sense wasting a clean pair of panties for bed when I'm on limited rations.

He wanders out of the bathroom with his skin still damp and a white towel wrapped around his waist, and my stomach does a little somersault at the sight of him. As he reaches the bed, he whips off his towel and starts to dry his hair with it, while I lie here looking at his magnificent body. When he's done, he pulls on a pair of boxers and lies down beside me.

"Are you wearing my clothes?" He arches an eyebrow at me.

"Yep. Because I've only brought a few pairs of clean panties and a few changes of clothes, and you have lots more than I do."

He lies back against the pillow with his arms behind his head. "What are we watching, Angel?"

"Some old movie with John Candy in," I shrug.

"Uncle Buck," he grins. "I love this."

We lie in silence for a while and I wonder why this seems slightly awkward between us, as though we didn't screw each other's brains out earlier in the basement of Ray's bar. Eventually, I can't take the tension any longer, and as funny as John Candy is, Uncle Buck just isn't doing it for me tonight. Rolling onto my side, I place my hand on Conor's chest. His muscles flex beneath my fingertips as he takes a deep breath. As I slide my hand down over his abs until they are dangerously close to his boxers, I nestle against him. "Are you nervous, Conor Ryan?" I purr as he groans softly and his cock twitches in his shorts.

"Yeah," he breathes.

I lift my head to look at him. "Really? With me? After everything we've done? After this morning?"

He reaches down and grabs me by the hips, pulling me on top of him until I'm straddling him and his semi-hard cock is nudging against my pussy. Placing my hands flat on his chest, I look down at him as he stares into my eyes. "This morning was incredible. But it happened so fast, I didn't have time to think about it. I was so fucking hot for you, I could barely think at all. And when I could, I was too busy worrying about how we were going to die in that fucking shit-box basement."

I press my lips together to stop from laughing out loud.

"But now I have you for the whole damn night, Angel, and I have thought about nothing but this for two long months. I wasn't even sure I'd ever get to do this again." His voice is thick with emotion and it makes my heart ache. I bite on my lip as I stare down at him.

"Aren't you wearing any panties?" He suddenly looks down at the space where our bodies join.

"No," I grin at him. "No sense in wasting a pair if I'm only going to wear them for a few hours, is it?"

"I suppose not." He arches at eyebrow at me. "But you are ruining my clean boxers with your cream, Angel. I haven't even touched you yet and I can feel it soaking through to my cock."

"Well, if you're worried about your clean underwear, you

should have thought this through like I did then, shouldn't you?" I tease him.

He narrows his eyes at me. "Take off the t-shirt. Right now," he growls.

"Okay," I breathe as I reach down and peel it over my head until I'm completely naked. Reaching up, he cups my heavy breasts in his hands and squeezes, making me groan as I press myself into his rough palms. "You kept this body away from me for too long, Angel."

"Then you shouldn't have told me to leave." I stare at him. He doesn't get to be the only injured party here. I've been hurting too.

He flips me over and pins me beneath him so fast my heart skips a beat, and I giggle. "I hope you're not tired, because I'm going to make up for every night you've been away from me."

"Promises, promises," I say with a dramatic sigh.

"I want all of you, Jessie," he says, brushing my hair back from my face and staring into my eyes.

"You already have every single part of me, Conor Ryan."

He presses his lips over mine and wet heat rushes between my thighs as he kisses me so hard my lips feel bruised. One hand slides down my body until he's between my thighs. I open them wider for him, allowing him to brush his thick fingers between my folds. He groans into my mouth when he realizes just how wet I am for him.

"Fuck, Angel," he hisses, breaking our kiss. "I'm going to eat you alive." He trails soft kisses down my neck, over my breasts, sucking each nipple into his mouth and gently nibbling while his fingers toy with me, rubbing over my clit and slipping down to my entrance before he dips the tip of one finger in before starting the maddening cycle again. As his kisses flutter over my stomach, I press my hips against him. "Conor. I've missed you too. Stop teasing me," I pant.

"I'm savoring you, Angel, not teasing," he murmurs against my skin as his lips move even lower. I pull my fingers through his hair as he reaches the apex of my thighs. "This where you want me, Angel?" he growls.

"Yes," I pant as his lips brush over my clit, causing a rush of heat.

"Jesus. I almost forgot how sweet your pussy is, Jessie," he groans as he presses the flat of his tongue against my opening and licks the length of my folds before settling over my clit, grazing it with his teeth and nudging it with his tongue as he slides two fingers inside me, making me arch my back with the thrill of pleasure that shoots through me. Curling his fingers inside, he presses against my G-spot as he rims my clit with his tongue, bringing me to the edge so quickly that my head starts to spin and I see flashes of light when I close my eyes.

"Conor!" I shout as he tips me over the edge.

"I gave you that one for free, Angel. I'm going to make you work for the next one."

"Really?" I gasp.

"Really," he flashes me a wicked grin, and I can see that his beard is wet with my arousal. He spends the next twenty minutes taunting me relentlessly with his fingers and his tongue until I am almost crying as I plead with him to let me come. When he finally takes pity on me, the rush of blood to my groin and the torrent of my wet release almost makes me pass out. I don't even have time to recover when he is nestling himself between my thighs and driving his cock into me. The wet sounds reverberate around the small motel room and he growls his appreciation. "I have missed this pussy, Angel."

I wrap my legs around his waist as he takes my wrists and pins them beside my head. "You want hard or gentle?"

"Hard," I breathe. "I want everything you've got, big guy."

"Fuck, Jessie!" he groans as he rails into me, nailing me to the bed so hard that the cheap headboard ricochets off the wall and snaps in two.

CHAPTER 24

CONOR

I rub my hand over the warm, soft skin of Jessie's hip and she groans softly in her sleep and presses her beautiful ass against my cock.

"Morning, Angel," I whisper in her ear before trailing soft kisses down her neck and onto her shoulders.

"Morning, big guy," she purrs, reaching behind her and curling her fingers in my hair.

"You have no idea how much I've missed this."

"Missed what?" she giggles as I slip my hand over onto her stomach.

"Waking up with your skin against mine, Angel," I growl as my hand slides between her thighs. She opens them wider for me with a soft moan and my cock throbs against her ass. "This body is so fucking soft and hot," I slip two fingers between her folds and suck the air between my teeth. "And wet."

"I missed waking up with you too, Conor," she breathes as she rolls her hips, rubbing her ass over my cock.

"So why did you leave me, Angel?" I nip at her sensitive skin and push one of my fingers inside her dripping pussy.

"Because you and your brother told me to," she gasps out loud.

"Open wider," I growl in her ear and she lifts her thigh, hooking her leg back over mine and allowing the tip of my cock to slip inside her as I slide my finger out and work my way up to her clit.

"Conor," she groans as she tries to push back against me to take more of me, but I don't let her. She doesn't get all of me until I'm one hundred percent sure I have all of her.

"Why did you run away?" I ask again.

The muscles in her body tense as I keep teasing her clit and nudging my cock deeper inside her. "Because Shane told me to," she snaps. "And you did. I looked at you, and you…"

"I what?"

"You gave me that look. Like I should go. Don't try to pretend that you didn't, Conor," she pants as she tries to stay pissed at me while her body reacts to the pleasure my fingers are bringing her.

"But you knew there was a tracker in that car. You knew we would come for you. You knew we would never let you go, Angel." I slide in another inch as I press harder against her clit and drag my teeth along her shoulder blade.

"I didn't know any of that," she hisses. "Shane told me it would never be the same. That I would never be one of you."

"He was trying to buy some time with Alexei. You weren't supposed to do such a good job of running. But you disappeared off the face of the fucking earth, Angel."

"I thought you didn't want me," she groans as she tries to buck her hips against me. "I would never have left if I'd known you wanted me to stay."

"I want you more than I have ever wanted anything in my life, Jessie. I love you so fucking much, I felt like I was going to die when I couldn't find you. When I thought I'd never touch you again, I wanted to tear off my own skin. And now that I've found you, how do I know you'll never leave me again?"

"Because I love you too. Please, Conor?"

That is all I need to hear. I push my cock deep inside her and her walls squeeze me, pulling me in deeper and milking me as she moans my name. I suck on the spot beneath her ear that drives her crazy, tasting her sweet, salty skin as I bury myself inside her.

ONCE I HAVE FUCKED us both to a release, Jessie and I lie on the bed facing each other.

"You are fucking beautiful," I say, making her blush as I reach out and brush her hair from her face.

She raises an eyebrow at me. "You're high on cum."

"I probably am. But you are still the most beautiful woman I have ever known, Jessie Ryan. And you need to learn to take a compliment."

"Then thank you," she whispers.

"How did you manage to ditch that car so quickly?" I ask her. Shortly after she drove out of our apartment building, I drove right after her, but by the time I caught up with the car in Baltimore, Jessie was long gone.

"You do remember how nice that car was, right? It was easy to sell it on with no questions asked."

"But you didn't keep the Camaro you traded it for?"

"No, of course not. I had six cars before I finally settled on my old Mustang. She was a real beauty. Until you killed her, anyway."

I hold up my hands in surrender. "I did what I had to do, Angel. And I would do it one hundred times over, because it got you here with me, didn't it?"

She shuffles closer to me, placing her hand on the back of my neck. "I suppose so," she smiles. "I'm glad you busted my car and busted me out of Ray's bar."

"How long do you expect we could stay holed up in this motel before my brothers come looking for us?" I flash my eyebrows at her.

"Shall we try it and see?" she giggles. "Or we could just travel the whole of the States, staying in cheap motels and picking up bar jobs when we need to earn some cash?"

I slide my hand onto her ass, pressing her body closer to mine. "As long as I get to do this with you every day, I'm game for a life on the run, Angel."

"You would never leave your brothers," she purrs as she brings her face closer to mine and brushes her lips across my cheek.

"Neither would you," I remind her.

"True. But we can pretend for a few days, can't we?" She trails her fingertips over my chest.

"We can pretend anything you like, Angel," I whisper before I press my lips against hers. She opens her mouth and lets me slip my tongue inside and the blood rushes straight to my cock. I love this woman more than I could have ever dreamed possible, and while she's lying here with me like this, the rest of the world doesn't even exist.

CHAPTER 25

JESSIE

After lying in bed longer than we should have, we were late setting off again, so Conor has driven like a demon for the past hour and a half to try and make up some time. We figure driving eight hours a day will get us back to New York in four days and leave us plenty of time to rest in the evening.

As we drive along the highway, I flick through the radio channels, trying to find some decent music.

"No country!" Conor warns.

"But I love country," I pout.

"I've got something much better," he says with a grin as he takes his cell from the center console and pushes a few buttons before turning up the volume. "Do you remember this?" he grins at me as the sound of Ride It by DJ Regard fills the car.

A flush creeps over my cheeks. Of course I remember it. It's one of my favorite songs in the world and he and I danced to it one night at his club. It was so hot we were practically banging on the dance floor.

I settle back against the seat as the thumping bass vibrates through my body and I recall in vivid, Technicolor detail Conor's hands on my ass and his lips on my neck as he rubbed his thick cock against me. "Conor. Pull the car over!" I say sharply and he looks at me in alarm as he swerves to the side of the road.

"What?" he frowns.

Unclipping my seatbelt, I climb over onto his lap, feeling a powerful surge of heat between my thighs. I've only been with him for a little over twenty-four hours and he has already turned me back into a raging sex addict. I can't get enough of him.

"Oh?" he growls at me and then presses a button to push his seat back before unclipping his own belt. I reach down and unbutton his jeans and he lifts his hips so he can pull them down slightly to allow his impressive cock enough room to spring free.

"I fucking love these sexy little denim skirts you've started wearing, Angel," he chuckles as he reaches beneath my skirt and pulls my panties down my legs. I push myself up onto my knees and between us we manage to wriggle them off completely. Conor keeps hold of them and stuffs them into the pocket of his jeans. I look into his deep brown eyes and they are dark with lust. As I shift my hips closer to him, he lifts his hands to my hair, brushing it off my face before he leans forward and runs his teeth over the soft skin of my throat and sucks gently on a tender spot beneath my ear.

"Conor!" I groan loudly as I roll my hips over his cock, coating it with my slick arousal and whimpering at the friction as it rubs against my clit.

"Take it whenever you want it, Angel," he whispers against my ear. "I'll let you be in control just this once."

The music fills the car and the beat pulses through my body as I reach down and take his cock in my hand before guiding it into my hot entrance. I have no time for patience or for teasing him right now because I am desperate to feel him inside me. I sink low onto him and moan loudly at the absolute relief I experience when he fills my pussy so completely.

"Fuck! Jessie," he hisses as my walls squeeze around him. I'm on the edge already and we're barely even moving. He slips his hands under my skirt again and grabs hold of my hips, his fingertips pressing into my soft flesh. "Show me how much you want me, Angel. I want to watch you make yourself come on my cock."

"Conor," I breathe as I plant my hands on his muscular shoulders and start to ride him, just like the song lyrics tell me to, as it plays over and over on repeat. Pressing my forehead against his, I bite my lip as I watch him slowly lose control while I move my hips over him, sinking deeper and deeper as his huge cock stretches me wider and my arousal coats the two of us.

"Damn, Angel, you feel so good riding me. You're going to make me come too fast." He grinds out the words as he tries to hold off from his impending release. His breathing comes fast and heavy and his fingers dig further into my hips as he drops his head to my neck and begins to nuzzle at that perfect, sweet spot beneath my ear that he knows drives me crazy. I throw my head back and thank God for the tinted windows in this car because I am about to come right here on the side of the highway while cars pass by.

Conor knows my body far too well, and as soon as he realizes I am on the edge too, he pulls my hips down, holding me in place while he thrusts upwards into me.

"Oh, God," I gasp.

"You take my cock so fucking good, Jessie," he groans as the tip of his length rubs against that place deep inside me and a few seconds later my orgasm tears through my body, and I come with a violent shudder as I shout his name. Wrapping his arms around me, he holds me tight as I grind down further onto him and a moment later, he bites down on my neck as he finds his own release.

When we have both stopped trembling, he lifts his head and looks into my eyes. "I think this is going to have to be our song now," he chuckles softly.

"I guess it will," I smile at him. "I will never hear it again and not think of you."

He pulls my face to his and kisses me deeply while his cock still throbs in my pussy and I melt into him as he fucks my mouth with his skilled tongue.

"Damn, Angel," he groans when he eventually pulls back. "I could go again in about two minutes, but I think we need to get going before a cop stops by and I have to roll down this window. And if anyone were to get a glimpse of your beautiful pussy, I would have to kill them. Cop or no cop. So, even though I was intending on keeping these panties, I'm going to give them back to you because your bare pussy is far too distracting."

I smile as I climb off him. "Fine. I can't be having some poor cop's death on my conscience, can I? Besides, we need to make up time from this morning."

He pulls up his jeans and fishes my panties from his pocket before handing them to me. "Yeah, and that was your fault too."

"My fault?" I arch an eyebrow at him as I slide my underwear back on. "I seem to remember it was you who wouldn't let me get out of bed."

"Well, how the fuck am I supposed to do that when your naked ass is pressed up against me, Angel? We'll never make it home in time if you don't stop tempting me with this sexy body of yours."

I can't help but grin as I crawl back into my seat and Conor laughs as he starts up the engine.

CHAPTER 26

JESSIE

*A*fter we had spent another whole day driving, I persuaded Conor to take me to the dive bar across the street from our motel. We sit at a small table with a beer each and I smile widely at him, but he only rolls his eyes in response. There is a live band singing country, which he hates, but I love.

"Come dance with me," I say, standing up and reaching for his hand.

"I don't dance, Angel."

"You danced with me in the club that time."

"That was because the music was good. This is shit," he smiles before he takes a sip of his Bud.

"I'm going to dance on my own then." I walk backwards, dropping his hand as I do.

"Knock yourself out, Angel," he says with a wink.

I walk over to the dance floor and choose a spot directly in Conor's eye-line before I start to dance. The band are playing a cover of Body Like a Backroad and I sway my hips in time to the music. I'm aware of the two guys nearby and Conor's eyes are drawn to them momentarily, before they flicker back to me. He narrows his eyes in warning, and I bite my lip as I drop my ass to the floor and pop back up.

The two guys edge closer, until they are standing on either side of me, close enough that I can smell stale beer and cigarettes on their clothes and skin. I ignore them, keeping my eyes trained on my hot bodyguard.

"You shouldn't be dancing like that here on your own, darlin'," one of them says as he moves to stand in front of me, blocking Conor's view.

"Oh, and why is that?" I glare at him.

"Someone might take advantage of your sweet nature," he smirks at me, revealing a gold canine tooth.

"I'm pretty sure my boyfriend would have something to say about that." I nod toward Conor and they both turn and look at him. He looks so out of place in this bar. He is fucking beautiful and he is huge. Way bigger than any other guy in here. Beside all that, there is just something about him that oozes danger and violence. I guess my two new buddies see it too, as they slope away without another word.

I keep dancing and can't help but smile as Conor downs his beer and makes his way over to me. When he reaches me, he slides his hands onto my ass and pulls me close to him until our bodies are pressed tightly together. I have to crane my neck to look up at him, but he bends his head low, his lips brushing over my ear. "Don't think I don't know what you're trying to do, Angel," he whispers.

"And what's that, big guy?" I flutter my eyelashes at him.

"I can tell you're in the mood for a little danger tonight, but you can grind that beautiful ass as much as you like, and I'm still not going to punish you. I will fucking kill anyone who touches you, though."

The surge of heat between my thighs makes my knees buckle and the look in his eyes tells me he is well aware of it too. Even the thought of him punishing me makes me wet and desperate for him. He brushes the back of his knuckles over my cheek and I stifle a groan. "You want to stay in this shit-hole and dance? Or you want to come back to the motel and dance for me?" he growls.

I blink up at him. I can't deny that a part of me wants to stay in this bar and dance because I like this band and this music. But the prospect of what he will do to me once we're alone has me a hot, trembling mess. "Let's go," I whisper, and he winks at me before guiding me out of the bar.

As soon as we're back in the motel room, Conor kicks the door closed and pushes me up against the wall. He wraps one hand around my throat while the other reaches under my skirt and he tugs my panties to one side.

"You're dripping, Angel," he hisses as he slides two fingers through my folds.

"I know," I pant as I push my hips against his fingers. "Please, Conor. I need you inside me right now."

"You want to be fucked against the wall like a stray I just picked up in a bar?" he growls in my ear.

"Yes," I groan as he plunges his fingers inside me.

"Take out my cock," he orders and I do as he tells me, unzipping his fly and squeezing his hard shaft, making him groan loudly. I plant soft kisses on his neck and a growl rumbles through his chest and throat.

"Turn around," he hisses.

When I do as he asks, he pulls my tank top up and off over my head before tossing it into the corner of the room. His warm fingertips trail softly down my back before he unhooks my bra and pushes it over my shoulders, letting my heavy breasts fall free. Once my top half is bare, he reaches around to my front and unzips my skirt before pushing it down over my legs, hooking his thumbs beneath the waistband of my panties as his hands slide over my hips and pulling them off too. I step out of my clothes until I'm standing completely naked. His lips graze my back as he presses me against the wall. "You are fucking beautiful. Every guy in that damn bar wanted you," he growls against my skin.

"Conor," I pant as I lean back against him. He pulls me toward him and begins walking me across the room until we are standing in front of the dresser and the large mirror, with my back flush against his hard chest.

His powerful hands slide down the back of my thighs and then he lifts me and places me onto the wooden dresser so I'm kneeling directly in front of the mirror. Pressing his body against mine, he drags his teeth along my shoulder blade as his hands slide over my hips and between my thighs before he pulls them wide apart until I am spread open for him. I watch him in the mirror as one hand slides up to my throat and the other slips between my slick folds.

"You remember the first time I fucked you, Angel? Just like this?" he growls against my ear.

"Yes," I whimper, recalling the afternoon in the boutique when he had me try on clothes and underwear for him for hours until we could no longer keep our hands off each other. I am as desperate for his touch right now, needing him to sate this burning desire I have to have him inside me.

"You look so fucking beautiful when you come apart for me, Jessie. I want you to watch me fucking you. I want you to see how good you look when I make you come and know that no-one knows your body better than I do," he whispers as he starts to draw slow, teasing circles over my clit while he increases the pressure on my windpipe slightly.

"Conor. Please?" I groan as I grind my hips against his hand until he gives me what I want and slides one of his thick fingers inside me, coaxing a rush of intense wet heat from me.

"Watching all those jackasses looking at you tonight made me so fucking hard, Angel. Seeing how much they wanted you and knowing they could never have you made me want to fuck you right in the middle of that dance floor." His hand on my throat slips down to my breasts, and he squeezes one roughly. "Who do you belong to?" he hisses, as he adds a second finger to my wet entrance.

"You," I breathe.

"Hmm," he mumbles against my skin. "And if you ever let any man other than my brothers touch you, I will fucking kill him. You got that?"

"Yes," I gasp as the warmth spreads through my thighs and stomach. As if he wasn't already hot enough, this possessive side of him makes me practically pant with need.

"This is mine, Jessie," he snarls as he slips his fingers out of me and palms my pussy roughly. "Mine," he repeats just before he bites down on my shoulder.

"Yours," I agree.

"Now look in that mirror and watch me fuck you," he says as he shifts himself between my thighs and nudges the end of his cock into my entrance. I drag my eyes to meet his in his reflection and the fire in them almost takes my breath away.

He tugs on one of my nipples and pinches my clit between two fingers just as he drives his cock into me, and I cry out in pleasure. "You feel that, Angel? I fit inside you so fucking perfectly. Your pussy was made for my cock."

I love this side of him so much. The filthy talking, possessive alpha that he doesn't let out very often back in the penthouse in New York. "Who do you belong to, Conor?" I purr.

He thrusts his hips harder, almost lifting me off the dresser as he rails into me. "You, Angel. Only you. Always."

AFTER HE HAS FUCKED me for the second time tonight, I lie on the bed, tracing my fingers over Conor's chest and down to his abdomen. "Why won't you punish me?" I whisper.

He sighs deeply and grabs hold of my hand, lacing his fingers with mine. "I want to be everything you need, Angel. And I would love to put you over my knee and spank that incredible ass. Or tie you to my bed and stripe your skin with my belt. But I don't want to hurt you."

"But I like a little pain," I remind him.

"I think you like more than a little, Jessie, and that's the problem."

I lean up on my elbow. "I don't understand," I say and he turns to face me.

"I love the way we fuck. I don't want to lose that. And I'm scared of losing control with you, Angel. That first time we had sex in my room, I tied you up, and I spanked your ass. Hard. And you fucking giggled, Jessie."

"Sorry," I blush.

He shakes his head and laughs softly. "I don't want you to apologize. You didn't hurt my feelings, but, you scared me."

"Why?"

He takes a deep breath. "When I was a little kid, I hated violence. I was terrified of my father and the beatings he used to give me and Shane, not to mention my poor mum. The sight of blood used to make me feel sick. But when I was eleven, my father made me start bare knuckle fighting. I pretty much sucked when I first started out, but if I wanted to avoid getting my ass kicked every week, I had to learn to get used to it. So, I did. And I got real good at it too. You saw me in that basement back in New York. You saw what I did to those men. To do that, I have to go to a place where nothing can touch me, Jessie. And I can't do that with you."

I lean forward and press a soft kiss against his temple. "I could reach you when you're in that place, though. You would never hurt me. I trust you."

He smiles at me and brushes his fingertips lightly over my cheek. "But I don't trust you, Angel."

His words are like a knife twisting in my heart and I try to shrink back from him, but he is too quick. Slipping his arm back around my waist, he holds me close. "How can you say that?" I blink at him.

"Don't get upset. I trust you with my life and my darkest secrets, but I don't trust that you'd tell me when you've had enough. I'm not sure you'd even know when you've had enough. And if I went to that place and you didn't pull me out, I might really hurt you, and I would never forgive myself. I couldn't stand for you to look at me after that."

"You think I don't know how much pain I can take?" I snap, unable to hide my annoyance.

"I think there is a difference between how much pain you can take and how much I'd be willing to give you. Or how much you need. I'm pretty sure you can handle a hell of a lot of pain, Angel." He runs his hand down to my ass and squeezes softly. "And that's why I won't go there with you. Not yet."

"But you might one day?"

"Maybe," he shrugs. "When you appreciate what your limits are."

"And how will you know that, though?" I arch an eyebrow at him. "If you think I'd let you push me too far, how could you be sure when I know what my limits are?"

He leans down and dusts his lips across my cheek. "Because Shane will tell me," he chuckles softly. "He's desperate to see how far he can push you."

"So you think it's okay for him to punish me, but not you?"

"Yep," he nods. "Because he loves spanking your ass. And there is no danger of him losing control with you. Not like that, anyway."

"Do you guys talk about me?"

Conor grins at me. "Course we do."

"Like, really talk? About what we do and stuff?"

He stares at me for a little while as though he's thinking about his answer, and my heart flutters in my chest. I mean, all of his brothers have watched me with each of them at some point, however talking about what we do privately seems a step too far. But then Conor's face breaks into a grin and he pulls me closer to him. "Don't look so worried. We don't talk about that stuff. Of course we talk about you though, just like we talk about each other. Shane knows you. He knows me. And he knows what you need, just like I do. He'll tell me when you're ready."

I close my eyes and press my head against Conor's chest, and I can't help but think about Shane and the time he punished me with his belt. He did push me to the edge of my limits, but then he sent me away, all hot and needy for him. Afterwards, he promised me that the next time it happened, it would end the right way, with him inside me. So despite the fact I am lying completely sated in Conor's arms, the thought of a spanking from his older brother still makes my pussy contract in anticipation.

CHAPTER 27

CONOR

I roll onto my side and press myself against Jessie's warm body. She moans softly in her sleep and wiggles her perfect ass against me. I will never get used to waking up next to her. She makes me feel like I'm invincible.

"Your boner is poking me in the ass," she says with a chuckle that makes my cock twitch.

"I can't help waking up like this when you're lying naked next to me, Angel," I say quietly in her ear. "Now stop wriggling or he'll be doing more than poking you."

"I think we need to pace ourselves, big guy, or I won't be able to walk by the time we get back to New York." She laughs again and I press my lips against her neck.

"You're really not helping," I growl.

She rolls onto her back until she's staring up at me. "Let's talk about something else then?"

"Okay. Tell me what you got up to during the two months I was looking for you."

She rolls her lips together and flutters her eyelashes at me in that way she does that makes me want to fuck her mouth.

I lean on my elbow so I'm looking down at her beautiful face.

SADIE KINCAID

Tracing my fingertips over her breasts and down onto her stomach, I smile as I watch her shiver beneath my touch. "Well?"

"I didn't get up to much at all," she shrugs. "I moved around a little, selling the cars I had bought on to new owners so that anyone looking for me would end up on a wild goose chase."

"Well, you certainly achieved that, Angel," I fake scowl at her, recalling the two months I trawled half the States looking for her.

"I'm sorry," she whispers. "But I was obviously sloppy somewhere. I must have left a breadcrumb for you to find."

"Hmm," I smile now. "I was chasing my tail until I found that guy you sold the Chevy to."

"Why?"

"He told me a brunette with an Irish accent sold him the car, so I ruled you out. But then he mentioned that you left a copy of Tolstoy in the glove compartment."

"That's how you found me?"

"Yeah."

"A breadcrumb only you could find," she smiles at me and the blood rushes to my dick.

"So, what did you do then? How long were you in Arizona?"

"Six weeks."

"And?" I raise my eyebrows at her.

"And, not much. I got that job in Ray's bar after two days. I found that little apartment and paid three months' rent with the leftover money from the SUV. I worked and then I went home."

"That was it?"

"Yes. It was pretty boring, but I liked it."

I reach up and tuck a strand of hair behind her ear. "But you hate being bored?"

She raises an eyebrow at me. "Jessie Heaton hated being bored. Ryan Smith quite liked it," she shrugs. "I don't know. I guess I wanted to be a completely different person. I didn't even have a smart phone."

"It kinda seemed like you didn't have a lot of money? That place you were living at? Working in that bar?"

"I don't have money," she says softly.

I frown at her because I can't comprehend how someone with her talent isn't sitting on a secret fortune.

"What?" she whispers. "You know Shane didn't leave that half of a million dollars lying around in that SUV, right?"

"I know that. But you've worked for some of the richest people in New York. You're the best at what you do. I guess I don't understand why you're so broke?" I grin at her because I don't want that to sound like an accusation.

"Well, money isn't really that important to me. Besides, it draws attention. People notice you when you're rich and I kind of like being unnoticed."

"You could never go unnoticed, Angel," I say, brushing my hand over her cheek and leaning down to steal a quick kiss.

She smiles back at me. "You know what I mean." She pushes gently against my chest. "Besides, I know how to get money if I ever really need it, and I suppose there is some security in that. There are plenty of billionaires with fat, off-shore bank accounts that I could tap into whenever I need to. And as for those rich people I worked for, it's not like Nikolai Semenov paid me for my services. And that was fine by me because I always had an ulterior motive."

"And we didn't pay you either," I add, feeling guilty at that realization.

"You gave me room and board, and everything else I ever needed," she purrs softly.

"So, you didn't look into Alexei at all?"

She shakes her head. "Not once. I suppose I was trying to convince myself if I didn't think about him, or any of it, I could really be this new person. I know it sounds crazy now, and I know it wouldn't have lasted, but it was nice to be normal for a little while. You know?"

"I get that, Angel."

"I should probably get a new laptop," she shrugs.

"We'll stop by somewhere and get you one today. Okay?"

"Yeah. Thank you."

"And what about guys?" I ask as my hand slides lower again and a wave of anger and jealousy rolls into my chest at the thought of anyone but me and my brothers putting their hands on her.

"I told you there was no-one else," she purrs.

"Some must have tried, though? I mean, you're hotter than fire, Jessie Ryan."

A blush creeps over her cheeks and she blinks at me. "A few asked me out, but I told them to go to hell."

Leaning down, I brush my lips over her cheek and the smell of her skin makes my cock throb. "You did, huh?"

"Yes," she breathes. "I much preferred my own company."

Fuck! "And who did you think about when you were getting yourself off then, Angel!" I growl as I press soft kisses along her jawline and onto her neck.

"Your brothers," she giggles.

"My brothers? Really?" I growl as I slide my hand between her thighs and rub two fingers softly over her clit.

"And you of course, and those magic fingers of yours." I slide my fingers lower until they reach her hot entrance. "Conor," she groans and winces slightly as I push a finger inside her.

"You sore this morning, Angel?"

"Yes. A little," she murmurs.

I grind my cock against her hip. "I need some part of me inside you, Jessie," I growl. "You think you can handle my mouth?"

"Yes," she gasps as I slide my finger out of her pussy.

"Come up here and sit on my face then?"

She grins at me as she sits up, scooting up the bed until she is straddling my face.

"I said sit, Jessie!"

"I am sitting," she protests.

Wrapping my arms around her thighs, I prepare to pull her down and hold her in place. "No. If I have to lift my head even half an inch for my lips to be touching yours, then you're not sitting, Angel. You're hovering. Now sit that beautiful pussy on my face now."

"What if I suffocate you?" She pops one eyebrow at me.

"Then I'll die a very fucking happy man! Now sit!" I pull her down onto my face as soon as the words have left my mouth and my cock throbs appreciatively as I taste her. "You're so fucking sweet," I mumble against her as I run my tongue the length of her pussy lips before sucking on her clit. She rides my face as I suck and lick at her delicious cunt and the sound of her whimpering and moaning my name makes me as hard as iron. She holds onto the headboard as she gets closer to the edge, until she's coming apart in my mouth.

I wipe my mouth as she climbs off me and grin up at her. "You are fucking delicious."

"Hmmm," she purrs contentedly. "I think you have a magic tongue too." She flashes me a wicked grin as she shifts down the bed and bends her head low until her lips are just inches from my cock.

"I'm pretty sure you can work some magic yourself." I flash my eyebrows at her and she grins at me before she grabs hold of my cock and licks the pre-cum from the tip, and the look of pleasure on her face makes my balls draw up into my stomach.

Jessie gives head like she enjoys it as much as I do and it's such a fucking turn on to watch her while she sucks my cock. She bobs her head and takes me all the way into her mouth until I'm nudging against her throat and the groan of pleasure rumbles through my body. If my tongue is magic, then hers is fucking miraculous. She runs it along my shaft as she sucks me greedily while she massages my balls, making me feel like a teenage boy when a few minutes later I spurt hot and heavy against the back of her throat.

The sounds she makes as she sucks me clean give me a warm feeling in the pit of my stomach. I lie back and smile as she crawls back up the bed and nestles herself against my chest. I love this woman more than I have ever loved anyone in my life.

CHAPTER 28

JESSIE

I leave Conor in the motel room talking on the phone to Shane while I go to reception to check out. They were discussing some business in Ireland that seemed to involve Shane's ex-fiancée, Erin, and I didn't want to hang around and listen to any conversation involving her. She brings out a jealous streak in me I didn't even know I had until I met the Ryan brothers.

After handing in our room key, I push open the doors of the motel reception and walk around the building to the parking lot where Conor's car is parked up, almost bumping into two men as I round the corner. One of them nudges the other and they share a look like they know me. I try to step past them, but they block my path.

"Hey, you're the girl from last night?" one says and I recognize them as the two men from the bar.

"Yeah! The cock-tease who shook her ass like a whore and then pretended she didn't want us to touch her," the other one adds.

I take a deep breath and count to five in my head. These are two big guys and while I'm pretty sure I could take one of them if

SADIE KINCAID

I caught him by surprise, both of them might be a stretch. As Conor is in the motel room talking to Shane, I could do without riling these assholes any further, so I resist the urge to make a snappy comeback. "Can you let a lady past please, gents?" I say with as sweet a smile as I can muster.

"You ain't no lady. Tramp!" the bearded one snorts and his buddy starts to laugh loudly and I see the flash of his gold canine tooth.

I shake my head and try to move past them again, but they move as I do, blocking my path to the front and side and preventing me from walking away.

"Guys? Please?" I say with a sigh.

"Please?" one says in a whiny voice as they both edge closer to me until I feel the heat from their bodies. Anger bubbles up from the pit of my stomach and comes out of my mouth before I can stop it.

"Why don't you pair of dickless wonders crawl back under whatever rock you slithered out from under and let me be on my way?" I snarl.

"Dickless?" The bearded one snarls as he grabs his crotch. "I'll show you dickless, bitch."

He grabs hold of my left arm and I swing my right one back and punch him in the jaw, making him stagger backwards. His buddy steps in and grabs me from behind, pinning both hands behind my back. "You gonna take that from this little whore, John?" he laughs as I try to wrench myself from his grip. But he holds me tight, his thick, sausage fingers digging into the soft flesh of my arms.

"Bitch!" The one I now know is John snarls as he wipes some blood from his mouth and steps back toward me. I stamp my foot down on the toes of the one holding me and he cries out in pain, but he doesn't let me go. Instead, he holds me tighter as John pushes his face close to mine. "Whores like you need to be taught a lesson, darlin,'" he leers at me as his hands drop to his cock

134

again. "Get her in the truck. Quick," he hisses as he looks around the empty parking lot.

"The fuck you will," I growl before I spit in his face. He raises his hand and slaps me hard across the cheek with the back of it, making my head snap back. Running my tongue over the inside of my cheek, I taste blood and I spit at him again.

"Fucking hell, Jeff. Muzzle her, will you?" he snarls at his buddy standing behind me and a few seconds later, a large, sweaty hand clamps over my mouth. "You need to be taught some manners, little girl," he says as he nods toward the truck and Jeff starts to walk me toward it.

I try to scream, but Jeff's grubby palm muffles the sound. I kick and wriggle as they drag me to the truck, but Jeff carries me with ease. I glance around, desperate for someone to see me. Where the hell is Conor? This isn't playtime any more. These two psychopaths are seriously going to kidnap me. Fuck!

My heart starts pounding in my chest as my eyes search for a weapon or something I can use to my advantage. John opens the truck door and Jeff lifts me by my waist with my arms still pinned behind my back. He is about to throw me onto the back seat but I plant my two feet on either side of the door frame to stop him.

"Get her the fuck in there," John hisses, as he quickly looks around us.

"Help me the fuck out then," Jeff snarls his reply.

John grabs hold of my legs by my knees, forcing them together to try and release them from the door frame. "Come on darlin'. I promise these legs will be spread wide for the rest of the day and night. But I need to get you in this truck first."

Jeff chuckles behind me. 'We're going to tear you apart, little girl,' he says against my ear and bile surges up my throat from my stomach.

"Not if I tear you apart first, you sick fuck!" I hear Conor's familiar growl behind me and almost cry with relief. He grabs hold of John first, pulling him away from me and punching him so hard in the face that he knocks him out cold.

Jeff releases me, turning to face Conor, who glares at him with a murderous look on his face.

"I'm going to rip off every part of your body that you touched her with," he snarls, his teeth bared like a rabid dog. "And then I'm going to make you beg for your momma while my girl watches me torture you to death."

Jeff's face turns a deathly shade of white, but he throws a punch at Conor, who ducks it easily, before he punches Jeff in the face, causing his nose to burst open like a ripe peach. Jeff howls in pain and drops to the floor as Conor starts raining blows down on his head. Although there is no doubt Jeff deserves whatever Conor has planned for him, I just want to get out of here. I look up to see two men walking out of the bar across the street and wonder if they might be buddies of John and Jeff.

I grab hold of Conor's arm. "Conor. Please stop. You'll only draw attention to us. This isn't New York. If someone calls the cops, they'll arrest us both. You've made your point. Let's go."

He turns to me, his eyes narrowed. "They were about to put you in their truck, Jessie. They were going to rape and probably kill you! They are going to fucking die for putting their hands on you."

"I know they deserve to, but I really want to go. Please?" I glance across the street at the two approaching men before I look back to Conor.

"For fuck's sake," he snarls as he takes his cell out of his pocket and snaps a picture of the number plate before taking my hand and walking us to his SUV. He picks up our bags from the floor on the way, which he must have dropped when he saw me almost being thrown into that truck.

"Why did you take a picture?" I whisper.

"You think I'm going to let them away with what they just did to you, Angel. I won't kill them, but I'll make damn sure someone else does. They will never put their hands on anyone else ever again. Now get in the goddamn car," he snaps and I climb inside with a lump in my throat. It seems like he's mad at me.

Once he's put our bags in the trunk, he jumps into the driver's seat. Reaching out his hand, he rubs the pad of his thumb over my lip. "Please let me go back there and fuck them up," he breathes.

Turning around, I see the two guys from the bar are now helping John and Jeff get to their feet. I have no doubt that Conor could take all four of them, but I don't want to hang around and have him prove my point. "I just want to get out of here, Conor. Please?"

He frowns and starts the ignition, before gunning the engine and wheel spinning out of the parking lot.

I sit in the passenger seat in silence as Conor glares at the road ahead. When we've driven about a mile, he pulls the car over and takes off his seatbelt before unclipping mine too. "Come here," he orders and I blink at him for a few seconds before I climb out of my seat and move onto his lap until I'm straddling him.

He draws in a deep breath and brushes my hair back from my face. "Are you hurt?"

"My cheek stings a little. But I'm okay. Why do guys like that think that they have a right to put their hands on women that way? Assholes!" I rub my cheek as though I can rub the stain of their hands from me, and he takes my hand and kisses my fingertips. Then he brushes his fingers over the mark on my face, much gentler than I did.

"Because they're backwards thinking, misogynistic assholes, Angel."

"They called me a cock teasing whore," I whisper. "Because I was dancing last night."

His whole body tenses beneath me. "Fuckers! You should have

let me deal with them. I would rip their fucking limbs off and shove them up their asses!" he snarls.

"They're not worth us getting into any trouble for, Conor. The last thing we need is to draw any unwanted attention to ourselves. I just want us to get home." I place my hands on his chest and his breathing slows.

"Home?" he smiles at me.

"You know what I mean," I whisper.

"But it is your home, Angel. I'm just happy to hear you calling it that again."

"I'm happy to be calling it that too," I say as I lean forward and place a soft kiss on his lips.

"How do you manage to have me eating out of the palm of your hand, Angel?" he breathes. "You have a power over me like no-one has ever had before."

I bite my lip as I look into his warm brown eyes. "That's not true."

"Yes, it is, and you know it. I would do anything for you, Jessie Ryan. You're all I think about every second of every day."

Wrapping my arms around his neck, I press a soft kiss against his cheek. "I love you, Conor Ryan," I breathe. "And I would do anything for you, too."

CHAPTER 29

CONOR

I lean against the doorway of the gas station with my cell phone to my ear as I watch Jessie choosing candy from the shelves. Shane answers my call on the third ring.

"Hey, Con. Everything okay?" he says.

"Yeah. And no. I'm going to send you a license plate after I end this call."

"Okay?"

"These two guys tried to take Jessie."

"Take her? What do you mean, take her?" he snaps and I can picture him frowning while he sits at his desk.

I peer through the door to make sure she's still there, and she smiles at me as she holds up a huge bag of candy. I shake my head and she pouts before putting it back on the shelf. "I mean like kidnap and rape her."

"What?" he shouts. "What the fuck happened? If you're sending me a plate then I assume they're still breathing? So why is that?" he snarls.

"They were two assholes from a bar we were in. They are still breathing because she just wanted to get out of there and begged me not to hang around and beat the two cunts to death."

"Fuck! Is she okay?"

"Yeah. She has a mark on her face, but she's okay."

I hear a sharp intake of breath before he answers. "Send me the picture and I'll make sure they're dealt with."

"Thanks."

"Rape and kidnap her?"

"Yeah." I swallow as I imagine what might have happened if I hadn't got to her when I did. "Our girl is a magnet for assholes."

"Well, I'll make sure they suffer then."

"You got any news at all on Alexei yet?" I keep my eyes on Jessie as she walks to the cash register to pay.

"No. Has Jessie got any idea where he might be?"

"No. We talked about him and she hasn't looked for him at all since she left. She's been completely off grid."

"I could really use her fucking help finding him, Con."

"I know. We'll be passing by a mall later today. We're going to stop off and get her a laptop. Once she's all set up, I'm sure she'll find him in no time."

"Yeah, well I hope so. Because as soon as he knows we have her, he's going to be back here with a fucking army."

"Yup. You thought about if maybe we should get out of the city for a while?"

"No!" he barks. "I'm not being driven out of our city by the fucking Russians."

"I know, but if it protects Jessie."

"We'll protect Jessie. He'll never lay another finger on her."

"You're right." I nod my agreement, although trouble has a habit of finding our girl even when she's not looking for it. "You heard any more about the evil cunt who spawned us?"

"No."

"How are Liam and Mikey?"

"Mikey's okay. But Liam is… well, you know how he gets. He's too hard on himself."

"Yeah, I know. Tell him Jessie will give him a video call later. That should cheer him up."

Shane laughs softly. "I'm sure it will."

"You want a call too, bro?"

"No. What I need to say should be said face to face," he says with a sigh.

"Okay. She misses you though."

"I gotta go," he says, clearly changing the subject. "Send me that license plate and I'll speak to you tomorrow."

"Okay. Bye."

Jessie walks through the door as I finish the call. "Everything okay?" she asks with a smile that damn near takes my breath away.

"Yup. Just checking in back home. Now let's hit the road and go find you a new laptop." I put my arm around her shoulder and we walk back to my car.

CHAPTER 30

JESSIE

*W*rapping a towel around myself, I step out of the bathroom to see Conor is still fiddling with the laptop he bought me earlier.

"I thought you might have joined me." I arch an eyebrow as I walk toward him.

He reaches out and pulls me onto his lap, rubbing his nose along my throat and inhaling deeply. "You smell incredible, Angel. And if you wanted me to join you, you should have asked. I thought you wanted me to get this thing up and running?"

"Have you?"

"Yep. And I've installed all of your apps from the cloud. You're good to go."

"Shall we video-call the twins now? You promised them a call, didn't you? And then we can just relax for the rest of the evening?"

"Relax?" he growls as he runs his hand up my thigh. "I have no intention of relaxing, Angel."

"Well, we'll be in bed at least," I say as I bite my lip.

He gives an exaggerated groan. "You'd better call them now then. You're connected to the WiFi."

Leaning forward, I open up the FaceTime app and dial Liam's number. He answers on the fourth ring. "Hey, baby," he grins as his handsome face fills the screen.

"Hey, Red," Mikey says as he nudges Liam out of the way.

"Umm, I am here too," Conor adds with a wave and a grin.

"We're not interested in you, bro," Liam laughs. "In fact, haven't you got to go out for half an hour? We want some time alone with our girl."

Conor tightens his grip on my waist. "Not a chance, boys."

Mikey and Liam grumble and complain and I can't help but laugh. "We'll be back in a few days, then you can have me all to yourselves," I say with a smile.

"Are you only wearing a towel, Red?" Mikey says as he brings his face closer to the screen.

"Yeah. I just got out of the shower."

He groans loudly. "Fuck. You're such a tease. Take it off!"

I tense instinctively at the word tease after those two assholes this morning, but I know Mikey means nothing by it, and there is no way he would ever disrespect a woman like that.

Conor obviously feels my reaction, and he kisses me softly on the shoulder as he rubs a hand over my hip and I melt against his chest. Then he reaches for the screen and tilts it slightly so his brothers can see my thighs. Or more likely, his hand sliding between them. "Say goodnight, gents. We got things to do here," he chuckles.

"If what you're doing involves your hand sliding up any further, I think it's only fair that you leave the camera on," Liam says in all seriousness.

I look up at Conor who flashes his eyebrows at me. "You want to watch me fucking our girl, boys?" he says in that smooth, velvety voice that turns my insides to jelly.

"What?" I say, shaking my head.

"We've watched you in real life, Red. Why not on the computer screen?"

I look between the twins on the screen and Conor, and they all seem to be totally up for this. I suppose Mikey has a point about them watching me before. "You wouldn't record it, would you?" I ask.

"And risk someone seeing our girl being fucked in the ass? No way," Mikey laughs.

"Who said the ass?" I gasp.

Conor laughs and shakes his head. "Hey, it wasn't me, Angel."

"Whatever you two feel like doing is fine with us. As long as we get to watch it all," Liam says as he nudges Mikey away from the screen.

"You sure you want to do this?" Conor rubs his hand over my back and nuzzles my neck.

"Yes," I breathe because the prospect of him fucking me while his brothers watch from thousands of miles away is so damn hot.

"Come on, then." He taps me on the ass and I stand as he picks up the laptop and places it on the nightstand. He turns to me with a look of deviance in his eyes and beckons me toward him. I step closer and he reaches up and pulls off my towel until I'm standing entirely naked.

"You're fucking beautiful, you know that?" he growls as his hands run over my body, while Liam and Mikey mumble their agreement. His hand slips between my thighs and he dips one finger inside me, making my legs tremble. Reaching out, I hold on to his shoulders as he quickly slides in another finger and I moan out loud.

"Fuck, Con," Mikey groans loudly making Conor chuckle before he withdrawing his hand. "Lie on the bed, Angel," he growls as he holds his fingers up and sucks them clean.

I step backwards and lie down as I look up at him while being acutely aware of Mikey and Liam watching us on the computer screen.

"How does she taste, bro?" Liam asks.

"As fucking sweet as you remember, but I'm not doing a

running commentary here, boys," Conor says as he undresses. "So stop asking questions and just sit back and enjoy the show."

When he's naked, Conor crawls onto the bed over me, holding himself up on his forearms and nudging my thighs apart with his knee. "Shall we give the boys a show that will keep them satisfied until we get back, Angel?" he whispers in my ear.

"Yes, please."

He trails kisses down my body until he settles between my thighs and for the next half hour he makes me come over and over again with his tongue and his fingers while his younger brothers watch from the side-lines. They encourage him on whenever I'm close to the edge and voice their approval each time he makes me come. When he finally pushes his cock inside me, I am beyond desperate to feel him. My walls clench around him as I pull him in deeper.

"Conor," I pant in his ear.

He growls against my neck, but it's the sound of the twins shouting and groaning that fills the room. "I think we just made my little brothers come, Angel," he laughs softly.

"I think we did," I laugh too.

"Hold on," he pulls out of me and I groan at the loss of him.

Conor pushes himself up onto his knees and leans over to the computer. "Show's over for tonight, boys. I'm glad you enjoyed yourselves, but this next segment is for my eyes only. Say goodnight."

"Aw, Con!" the twins protest.

"Goodnight, boys," I shout to the screen before Conor presses the button to end the call.

He leans back over me and presses his lips against my ear as he nudges the tip of his cock against my entrance. "You're so fucking wet, Jessie."

"I know."

"I love fucking your pussy, but I want to fuck your ass."

My insides melt like butter. "Is that why you turned the laptop off?"

"Hmm," he mumbles against me and it vibrates over my skin, making me shiver. "I don't want those animals watching me the first time I fuck this juicy ass," he says as he takes hold of it and squeezes. Then he slides his hand to my pussy and dips a finger inside. "We don't have any lube, Angel, but I think we got enough of your cream here to do the job. What do you say?"

"Yes," I breathe.

Fire blazes in his eyes and he pushes himself up and climbs off the bed.

"You want me to flip over?" I arch an eyebrow at him.

He shakes his head. "Nope." Then he reaches down and grabs me by the hips, pulling me to the edge of the bed as he drops to his knees. "This motel bed is the perfect height."

"Oh." I chew on my lip. I've never done it this way before.

Conor lifts my legs until my knees are hooked over his shoulders and my hips are slightly raised off the bed. His cock nudges at the seam of my ass. He was right. This is the perfect height. Slipping one of his hands between my thighs, he coats a finger in my juices before sliding it to my ass and pushing it inside up to his knuckle.

I groan loudly as I instinctively raise my hips. He places a firm hand on my abdomen, applying the perfect amount of pressure to keep me in place. "Your ass is so hot and tight," he growls as he slides his finger deeper inside. At the same time, he edges forward, lifting his hips and sliding his cock deep inside my wet pussy.

"Conor!"

"That good, Angel?" he hisses.

"Uh-huh," I nod as he finger fucks my ass while he gently thrusts in and out of me.

"You think my cock is slippery enough yet?" he chuckles and

heat sears across my cheeks because we both know that it is. I am dripping for him.

He withdraws his finger and his cock and I take a deep breath as I prepare for what's about to happen. He switches hands, using the fingers of the one he was pushing down on my abdomen with to slide through my slick folds as he pushes his cock into my ass. "Fuck, Jessie," he grinds out as he works the tip inside.

Instinctively, I tense my muscles and he sucks in a deep breath before he looks at me with a frown on his face. "You okay?"

"Yeah. I've just never done it like this before," I whisper. "It feels so much more intimate to be looking at your face while you're doing that."

"That's kind of the point, Angel."

I chew on my lip. "I know."

"Let's make you a little more comfortable then." He winks at me just as he slides two thick fingers deep inside my pussy.

"Oh, fuck," I groan as my back arches in pleasure. He presses his free hand down on my abdomen again, holding me in place as he finger fucks me, coaxing an intense rush of wet heat from me. It trickles down the seam of my ass, providing him with more lubricant. He takes the opportunity to slide his cock further inside and this time he meets no resistance. "That's it. Let me all the way inside you," he growls as he pushes deeper.

"Conor," I groan. "That feels so good."

"I know, Angel," he hisses. "I'm so desperate to fuck you."

"Then do it. Please!" I breathe as waves of pleasure roll over my body. He moves his hips slowly at first, allowing me to adjust to him while at the same time pumping his fingers in and out of my pussy. I close my eyes as the feelings of euphoria threaten to completely overwhelm me.

"Look at me, Jessie," he commands and my eyes fly open and lock on his. His eyes stay fixed on mine as he works my body expertly, bringing me to the edge of my limits before easing me back down again. When I feel like I can't take any more, he shifts his hand on my abdomen slightly lower, still holding me in place, but close enough that he can rub my clit with his thumb and I swear my eyes almost roll out of my head.

"Conor!" I half groan, half scream his name. He glares down at me with his dark, fiery eyes as he maintains his slow, steady pace and coaxes the longest, most intense orgasm from me. It releases a gush of fluid and he growls his appreciation.

As I blink up at him as a flush creeps over my cheeks. Only Shane has ever made that happen before, and I know how much he loves it, but I always feel a little embarrassed. However, Conor looks down at me with such love and desire burning through him that it makes me smile.

"That was fucking incredible," he growls, rubbing the last of my orgasm out with his fingers before he releases my legs, planting them on the floor as he leans over me. "I have no idea how I've stopped myself from coming yet," he says, pinning my hands to the bed.

"Neither do I," I pant. "Because that was something else."

"Wrap your legs around me," he whispers against my ear.

I do as he asks while he presses deeper into my ass. "I'm going to fuck you real hard now. Okay?"

"Okay," I breathe as he releases my hands and I snake my arms around him too. He seals his mouth over mine and kisses me hungrily. Then he fucks me so hard I almost pass out. When he finds his own release, he throws his head back. "Fuck, Jessie!" he growls like a wild animal as he fills me with his release.

He eases out gently and then he folds over me, his head resting on my breasts as he remains kneeling on the floor.

"I love you," I whisper as I curl his hair around my index finger.

He smiles against my skin. "Love you too, Angel."

. . .

After we've both showered again and eaten some food, Conor and I lie on the bed watching TV. My eyes are drawn to the laptop on the nightstand.

"You want to fire that up now?" he asks, cupping my chin and tilting my head so he can look at my face.

I shake my head.

"You sure?"

"I want one more day of pretending we're just a normal couple before I have to go back into that world. Is that okay?"

"Of course."

We lie there in silence, but that damn laptop is calling me. I refuse to switch it on, though. I refuse to spend the next few hours trawling the dark net trying to find Alexei.

"I assume he's no longer at his fortress in Connecticut?" I whisper.

Conor runs a warm hand over my arm. "No. Shane has been looking for him, but he's gone to ground again. We have no idea where he is."

"You understand he'll come for me as soon as he finds out I'm back in New York?"

"Yes."

"Are you all okay with that?"

"Of course we are. We'll be ready for him this time, Angel."

I sit up and shuffle back until I'm leaning against the headboard.

"You want to talk about it?" Conor asks.

I chew on my lip because the answer isn't so straightforward. "I don't want to. But, I'm not sure I can avoid it any longer."

He sits up too and puts an arm around my shoulder. "Okay. Let's start with what we already know" he suggests.

That sounds like a good idea. Perhaps putting things a little straighter in my head will stop my mind from racing for now. I take a deep breath. "Alexei and my father were twins. He believes he is my father though, and that my mom and dad stole me from him."

Conor nods. "And Alexei is the head of the Russian mob."

"You're certain of that?" I ask.

Conor nods. "One hundred percent. His identity has always been a closely guarded secret, but, well, when you disappeared with him, let's just say we turned over every stone we could to find out who he was."

I swallow, recalling the heartbreak I caused myself and the brothers, believing that Alexei was the father I had watched murdered by the Wolf, and leaving with him that day. As if reading my mind, Conor reaches up and strokes my cheek with the back of his knuckles.

"What else?" he whispers.

"We know that Alexei was married to my mom two years before I was born. And that her name was Nataliya then."

"But your mom left Russia when she was pregnant with you. And she changed her name to Veronica?"

I nod. "So, my mom was married to Alexei? But she fell for my dad? Or maybe she always wanted my dad?"

Conor nods his agreement. "Maybe."

"We know for sure that Alexei paid for the hit on my family and that the Wolf was supposed to deliver me to him, but decided to keep me for himself."

"Yeah."

"I wonder why, though? The Wolf was the Bratva's top assassin. Why would he risk his whole career for some girl? He defied the head of the Russian mob to keep me prisoner. I mean, I get what he wanted from me." I shudder at the memories and tears prick at my eyes. "But he was so powerful, I'm sure he could have had his pick from so many women."

Conor presses his lips against my forehead and his body tenses. "I will never let him hurt you again, Angel."

"I know."

"We will find Alexei and the Wolf, and we will make sure they give you the answers you need before we make them pay for everything they have ever taken from you."

"I'm not sure there's anything you could do to them that would make them pay for everything, Conor," I say as a shiver runs down my spine. A tear rolls down my cheek and Conor brushes it away with the pad of his thumb. "I don't know who I hate more. I suppose the Wolf was just doing his job, and if it wasn't for Alexei, I would still have my family. But the Wolf…" I shake my head. "He took everything I had left," I whisper.

"You are a fucking warrior, Jessie Ryan."

I don't want to think about the Wolf or Alexei Ivanov any more. "I like being a Ryan," I say with a smile.

He arches an eyebrow at me. "We could swing by Atlantic City on our way home and make you a Ryan for real?"

"As in get married? Are you serious?" I shove my hands against his chest. "The twins would kill us."

He laughs out loud. "Liam and Mikey would get over it eventually, as long as I agreed to share you, but Shane would cut off my balls."

"Why? Does he hate me that much?" I ask as my heart flutters in my chest. I don't think I will feel okay about anything until I can speak to him again. There were so many things we left unsaid. I will never forget the look in his eyes when he told me he would never forgive me for leaving them. He was right too. I had promised them all I would never leave. But I still did.

Conor cups my chin in his hand and leans closer to me. "No. He doesn't hate you at all. But I can't have this conversation with you, Angel, because I promised him that I wouldn't."

I blink at him. "What conversation?"

"This one. About you and him."

Closing my eyes, I snuggle into his chest. I don't imagine I will ever understand Shane Ryan.

"He's not the cold-hearted bastard you think he is, Angel," Conor says as he brushes my hair behind my ear.

"I know that," I say, because I don't think he's cold hearted at all. But he is as stubborn as a mule.

"He never wanted to come to New York, you know? He was happy back in Ireland."

I look up at him again. "Really. So, why did he?"

"Because of our father."

"Didn't he and Shane get on?"

"They did once. Shane was always our dad's favorite. In fact, he didn't want any more kids. He barely tolerated me, but he plain despised Liam and Mikey, and he made no attempt at hiding it either."

I sit up straighter again so I can look at his face. "Really?"

He nods. "Growing up, he was cruel and spiteful. Our mum tried to protect us as best she could, but she couldn't even protect herself. He killed her when I was nine. The twins were only one."

My hand flies to my mouth. I knew that there was a history with their father, but I had no idea it involved anything like this. "He killed her? Did he go to prison?"

Conor shakes his head and scowls. "Patrick Ryan rules Belfast, Jessie. He's Teflon. Invincible, and completely fucking untouchable. He told everyone she fell and hit her head and no-one dared to disagree with him. My mum had a sister, Em, and she tried to help. But she was no match for him. He drove her away just like he did his own brother. No matter what he ever did, he always walked away without a scratch."

"Wow!" I blink at him. "What happened to you all after she died?"

"We stayed with him. He was our dad and, as far as he was concerned, we were his property. Shane was thirteen, and he became our protector after that. He did a good job most of the time. But our dad decided I needed to start taking care of myself. No son of Patrick Ryan was going to let other people fight his battles. So, he started me bare-knuckle boxing. I was a weedy kid, believe it or not. Tall and skinny. I hated fighting. I came home every single week with a bloody nose or a broken bone, but he kept on sending me out there, fighting kids older and twice the size of me. He said it would build my character. And when I lost, he would give me a beating too, for being weak."

"Conor," I reach for him and take hold of his hand as my heart breaks for the little boy he was.

"Maybe he had a point because I sure as hell got good at winning pretty quick. I didn't have much choice. Shane taught me the most effective ways to disable guys twice my size, and I started to win all of my fights. Shane always stuck up for me at home, but I tried to stay out of my dad's way as much as possible. But then, the twins got older and, fuck, Shane spent almost every hour of every day having to look out for those poor little bastards." Conor shakes his head. "I swear our dad would have killed the two of them if it wasn't for Shane."

I have to take a deep breath as I think about the four wonderful men I know and what they must have endured at the hands of the man who was supposed to protect them. "God. You must have all been terrified of him?"

He nods.

"So what made you come to New York, though? Did something happen?"

Conor nods. "My dad only got worse as he got older, and we got bigger and stronger. The less able he became to physically control us, the crueler and more vicious he got. Particularly me and Shane. By the time I was sixteen, we could both kick his ass, and he knew neither of us were scared of him. But as he'd already taken our mum, he used the twins to keep us in line instead."

"Shit!"

"Yeah. He is a piece of work," Conor says as he looks beyond me and into the distance.

"He's still alive?"

"Unfortunately, yes. Although not for much longer. He's sick. Lung cancer. Apparently, he hasn't got long left. But death is too merciful for that fucker. Shane almost killed him the night before we came to the States, but, well that's Shane's story to tell, Angel, not mine."

"So you all came here to the States after that?"

"Yes, but not because Shane almost killed him. Because of why Shane tried to kill him."

"And why was that?"

"Hmm? Well, that one is the twins' story to tell," he arches an eyebrow at me.

I place my hands on his face. "I'm sorry you went through all that."

"Made me the man I am today," he says with a shrug.

CHAPTER 31

SHANE

I sit at my desk staring at the blank computer screen, so lost in my own thoughts that I don't even hear Liam walk into the room.

"You okay?" he asks quietly as he takes a seat opposite me.

"What?" I blink at him as he narrows his dark eyes at me in concern. "Yeah. Just thinking."

"Did I hear you on the phone to Aunt Em earlier?"

I nod in response. Our Aunt Emma is our mother's younger sister. She and her daughter, Siobhan, are the only members of our family in Ireland that we have any contact with. Emma did her best to look out for us when we were kids, but she was barely more than a kid herself. My father terrified her, as he does most people, and eventually he drove her away completely. We reconnected when me and my brothers moved to New York. She hates our father almost as much as we do.

"She give you any news?" Liam asks with a frown.

"He's still alive," I reply. "Barely."

His only response is a snort.

"Apparently, he's asking for us."

I see the change in Liam's face instantly as it contorts in pain and anger. "What?" he snarls. "All of us? Or just you?"

"All of us," I reply with a sigh. There is no escaping the fact that I have always been our father's favorite — a curse rather than a blessing.

"Cunt!" Liam spits. "Why? What has he said?"

"Em spoke to his nurse. She said he's been asking her to contact his sons for him. He told her he had four and they'd all moved away and left him. Seems this nurse is doing her best to get our contact details, but Em wouldn't give them up."

"Four sons?" Liam shouts before banging his fist on my desk. "Four? Did he conveniently forget he all but disowned me and Mikey the moment we were born?" He is unable to contain his anger and he slams his fist down on my desk. "He is no fucking father of mine!"

"I know." I reach across the desk and place my hand on top of his. The things our cunt of a father put my younger brothers through still give me nightmares and I can't imagine the horrors that even hearing his name bring up for Liam and Mikey.

He looks up at me with tears in his eyes and I have to force myself not to look away from him, because it kills me to see him like this. I haven't seen Liam cry since he was three years old and recalling that day slices a fresh welt across my heart. Mikey used to cry. It was a pitiful sound that used to cut through me like glass. But Liam never cried, because he understood from a very young age that his tears gave our father some sick sense of satisfaction.

He's twenty-six years old now and he is on the brink of breaking down in front of my eyes. "When you speak to Aunt Em again, you give her a message for that nurse of his," he spits. "You tell her that I am no fucking son of his. He gave up the right to call himself my father when he tried to drown me at birth, and every other fucking time he tried to kill me."

"I'll tell her," I say, squeezing his hand.

"Why did he fucking hate me so much, Shane?" He hangs his head low and sniffs loudly, trying to stop himself from crying.

"Because she loved you so fucking much, that's why." I place my free hand on top of his head. "Mum was over the fucking moon when she found out she was having twins and he hated that she wanted you so much. She hid everything from him as much as she could, but when he wasn't there, she would tell me and Conor about all her plans for you both. Her dreams for all of us. She used to let us feel her stomach whenever you kicked. He despised that he already had to share her with me and Conor, and he couldn't handle how much of her time and attention you needed. She named you both after her grandfathers. And he hated that too."

"Did he kill her because of us?" Liam sniffs.

"No! He killed her because he is a jealous, sadistic cunt, and don't ever forget that."

Liam wipes his cheeks with the back of his hand but keeps his head bent low because he doesn't want me to see his tears. As though I might think him weak, when he is one of the strongest men I have ever known.

"I don't even remember her," he whispers.

"I know, kid," I say as emotion almost chokes me. Our father murdered her when the twins were only a year old. I am both blessed and cursed by memories of her. She had a smile that could make you forget any hurt you felt. She had the softest hands. She was kind and smart and funny. She was everything our father was not. And despite everything he ever did to her, she always woke us each morning with a smile and a kiss on the forehead. "You remind me so much of her. The way you can make people see things differently. She could do that. Your eyes crinkle the same way as hers when you smile too," I say, swallowing the lump in my throat.

"He took everything from us," Liam spits.

I sit and look at my youngest brother and the guilt of what

happened the night before we left for New York weighs heavy on me. "I'm sorry I didn't kill him for you, kid."

He looks up at me and wipes his eyes with the pads of his thumbs. "What? That's not on you, Shane."

"It is," I swallow hard. I've never told Liam or Mikey this before. "The night before we left, I found him. He was at mum's grave. He was drunk. And alone. Crying about how much he missed her."

Liam frowns at me, but he doesn't speak.

"I pressed a gun against his head, Liam, and all I had to do was pull the trigger, but I couldn't do it. I couldn't let him die on her grave. Not after what he did to her. I couldn't tie him to her in death too." I feel the tear run down my own cheek and wipe it away. "But I should have dragged him out of there and put a bullet in his head for what he did to you and Mikey. I let you both down."

Liam stares at me for what seems like a goddamn eternity. He's always looked up to me. He's held me on some kind of pedestal, and I can't help but think I just knocked myself off it. "No," he finally answers with a vigorous shake of his head. "You didn't let us down. Not even for a second. You raised us, Shane. All of us. If it wasn't for you, none of us would have survived at all. You could kick our asses onto the street and never speak to us again for the rest of our lives and you'd still have done more for us than any brother could ever ask. I would still owe you everything."

"I didn't do anything that you wouldn't do for me," I say dismissively, uncomfortable with the fact that he thinks he owes me anything at all. For all I have done for my brothers, they have done just as much for me.

Liam smiles at me. "You say I can't take a compliment?"

"Well, I already know I'm awesome," I laugh. "And I did a pretty fucking good job of raising you, didn't I?"

Liam grins at me and I see the little kid who used to sneak

into my room in the middle of the night to make sure I hadn't left him. When I called off the wedding to Erin, she blamed my brothers. She couldn't accept the fact that it was due to her deceit and manipulation. And while she was wrong about a lot of things, she was right about the fact that I would never leave them. Not for anyone.

CHAPTER 32

MIKEY

"*Y*ou seen Liam anywhere?" I pop my head into Shane's office as I look for my twin.

"He was in here about an hour ago," Shane frowns. "Why? Can't you find him?"

"No." I shake my head as I step inside the room.

"You checked the gym?"

"Checked this whole damn apartment and the club."

"Fuck!" Shane hisses.

"What?" I frown at him.

"He was talking about mum before-"

"And the sadistic prick who we once called dad?" Mikey interrupts me.

"Yep."

"Shit. He'll be down by the river then. I'll go get him." Liam likes to go and sit by the Hudson when he's feeling particularly melancholy. He says it reminds him of Ireland, although why he wants to be reminded of the place I'll never know. It's a beautiful country, but our lives there were miserable.

"You want me to come with you?" Shane offers.

"Nah." I shake my head. "I'll bring him back."

"Call me if you need me," Shane frowns.

"Yeah, I will," I say as I turn on my heel.

"Mikey!" Shane shouts as I'm halfway out of the door.

"Yeah?" I turn back to him.

"Are you okay?" He narrows his eyes in concern.

"You know me, Shane. I'm good."

"Yeah, I do know you. So that's why I'm asking if you're okay?"

I walk into his office and sit on his desk. He does know me. Apart from my twin, Shane knows me better than anyone. He's always been my father really. Ever since he saved me and Liam from being drowned in a bathtub when we were a few hours old by the lunatic who actually spawned us. It was just one of the many times he saved our lives. "What else should I be? A man I hate, who hates me, who I barely know, and who lives on the other side of the world, is dying. It has no impact on my life really, does it?" I shrug.

"I suppose not when you put it like that."

"Liam is cut up though," I say because these past few days I have watched him become more and more withdrawn. The only time he has a smile on his face is when Jessie calls and I wish she'd hurry her ass up and get back to us, because I miss her like crazy too.

"I know."

"It's funny how he never feels good enough, isn't it? He's one of the best people I know, but he always doubts himself. Yet the most horrible bastard to ever walk this earth is sitting back in Ireland, riddled with disease, and yet still thinks he is the goddamn king of the world, when Liam is one hundred times the man he ever was."

"Yep," Shane nods. "But we're still talking about Liam and I asked how you were doing?"

"I told you," I snap.

"I don't believe you."

161

"I miss Jessie," I admit. "And I miss Conor too. Nothing's the same around here without them."

"They'll be back soon," he says and I see the change in him at the mention of her name.

"How are you, Shane?"

He frowns at me. "Fine."

"Don't believe you." I tilt my head as I watch him trying his best not to tell me to fuck off out of his office. "Don't like that, do you, bro?"

"Fuck off, Mikey," he says with a sigh.

I shake my head. He, of all people, doesn't deserve my attitude. The truth is, I've been completely off kilter since I found out our father was dying of cancer, because it has dredged up so many long buried memories. And all of the people I could talk to about it are hurting too. Except Jessie.

Fuck, I miss her so much. She would make it better even if she didn't realize that was what she was doing. Just watching TV with her or playing cards soothes my soul in a way that nothing else can.

"I'm sorry," I say to him. "But I know you're not fine, Shane. You try and hold everything together for everyone else, and you can't do that forever, bro. One day soon, something is going to give."

"Since when were you all deep and philosophical?" He narrows his green eyes at me.

I shake my head. "I mean it, Shane. You can't keep living like this, bro."

"Like what?" he scowls.

"Half a fucking life. Never letting anyone in."

"Is this about Jessie?" he says with a sigh.

"You tell me. Do you miss her?"

"Go and bring Liam back. You two have work to do," he says with a wave of his hand.

"Answer me and I'll go get our baby brother back," I challenge him.

"What the fuck, Mikey?" he shouts. "What the fuck do you want from me?"

I stand up from my chair. I don't want to fight with him, but he is the most stubborn bastard I have ever known. "It's just a question, Shane. Do you miss her?"

"Every minute of every damn day!" he shouts and I see the veneer of control he always hides behind slipping slightly. "Is that what you want to hear? That I can't go more than two minutes without thinking about her? Well, now you know. But it still doesn't change the fact that she tore my fucking heart out. Now, go and get Liam and get your asses back to work!" he snarls at me and I walk out of his office with his words ringing in my ears. Damn! I have never pushed his buttons like that before. And now I feel like shit for making him lose control because I know how much he hates it.

I walk down the hallway and press the button to the elevator as I prepare to go and find my twin and talk some sense into him. How is it that suddenly I am the sane one in this apartment?

I START the engine of my car and dial Conor's number.

"Hey, everything okay, bro?" he asks.

"I just made Shane really mad," I say with a sigh.

"Why? What did you do?"

"I made him talk about feelings."

"Ouch," Conor says with a laugh. "What the hell did you do that for?"

"He started it. Asking me how I'm doing." I suck in a deep breath.

"How are you doing, kid?" Conor asks.

"Don't you start, Con," I laugh to ease the tension because I'm not calling to have a heart to heart with him. In fact, I'm not calling him at all. "Can I talk to Jessie?"

"Sure. She's right here. I'll hand you over."

I wait for a few seconds until her sweet voice fills my ear. "Hi Mikey," she says and all the tension I didn't even realize I was holding in my chest and shoulders melts away.

"Hey, Red."

"You okay?"

"Are we on speaker?"

"No. Just me and you," she says softly. "Conor is watching TV. Is something wrong?"

"No. I just wanted to hear your voice. I miss you, Red."

"I miss you too," she says quietly. "We'll be home in a few days. I can't wait to see you. Are you sure everything's okay?"

"I made Shane really pissed at me," I admit as tears spring to my eyes completely unexpectedly.

"Well, that's not exactly difficult," she laughs softly but I know that she gets it because she gets me. "He won't stay mad at you for long. The two of you will be arguing over the Giants and the Jets before you know it."

"Ah, I don't know. I really pushed his buttons this time."

"What did you do?"

I can't tell her what I asked him about because I know she'll already be worried about facing him when she comes back here. I imagine that Conor has told her it will all be okay once she speaks to him and straightens it out, but I'm not sure it will be. Shane will have Jessie back in our home because the rest of us want her here so badly, but I'm not convinced that he is as thrilled at the prospect of her return as we are. "Just being an asshole. You know me."

"You're not an asshole!" she admonishes me. "Not even a little bit."

"Really?" I laugh.

"Well, except for that time at that wedding when you boinked the bride at the reception!" She starts to laugh and the sound warms me from the inside.

"Yeah, I was definitely an asshole that day," I laugh too. We spend the next few minutes chatting about nothing in particular as I drive through the streets of New York to Liam's favorite spot by the river. But talking to her makes me forget how angry I feel at the world and by the time I see Liam, sitting on his own, staring out over the Hudson, I feel like I could conquer the whole world again.

CHAPTER 33

SHANE

*L*iam and Mikey are walking through the elevator doors just as I'm heading out. Mikey sent me a text to let me know that he'd found him and he was fine, but it's still a relief to see him back here. I wrap my arms around his neck. "You okay?"

"Yeah," he says as he hugs me back.

"Good." I pull back from him. "You gonna be okay on your own downstairs tonight?"

He nods and I turn to Mikey. "I need you with me."

"Where are we going?" he asks with a worried look on his face.

"To break some faces," I wink at him and his face breaks into a grin.

"Aw. Why can't I come then?" Liam asks.

"Because someone needs to watch the club. And you've slacked off enough for today!"

"Fair enough," he replies with a roll of his eyes. "I'll just go get changed. You two don't have too much fun without me now."

"As if we would," Mikey says before we both step into the elevator.

We ride down to the basement and get into the car in silence. I feel Mikey's eyes burning into me as I drive out of the parking garage. "What?" I say as I turn to him.

"I'm sorry. You didn't deserve that. I felt like shit all day."

"Forget about it."

"Where are we going?"

"To find some assholes!"

"Yeah, well that narrows it down," Mikey laughs.

"Those pricks from Angelino's have been causing trouble again is all. I thought I'd pay them a visit. And now you are too."

"But isn't this like using a pneumatic drill to crack a walnut? Can't our bouncers deal with this?"

"Yes," I frown at him. "But I want to." It's true that dealing with some local low-life bouncers from a club in Brooklyn that is about a quarter the size of ours is way below our pay grade, but they have been bothering us for a while now, and it needs to be stamped out before it escalates. Besides, sometimes I just need to let off some steam.

"Oh, I see," Mikey says with a grin as he rubs his hands together expectantly. "I haven't done this with you for a long time."

"I know."

"I should push your buttons more often," he chuckles to himself.

"Don't!" I warn him.

A LITTLE OVER half an hour later, we pull up outside the club in Brooklyn. It's not open yet but the bouncers are already showing up for their shifts.

"What's it to be? Fists or we brought weapons?" Mikey asks.

"Some brass knuckles should do just fine," I wink at him as I nod to the glove box.

He takes out a brass knuckle with a blade on the end and

holds it up so the metal catches the light. "Nice. These new?"

"Conor got them a few months back. Hand me mine," I say and he reaches into the box and pulls out a second one. I slide it onto my right fist and we climb out of the car. The bouncers hanging around outside spot us as we walk over the road and they shout for their colleagues who walk around the side of the building.

"How many you think there are?" Mikey asks.

"At this time of night? Six, tops,"

"Then why do I count eight, bro?" he replies as another two come out from inside.

"Six? Eight? Who gives a shit?"

"Fuck me, you are in the mood for some fun, aren't you?" he chuckles to himself.

"Yep," I nod as I start to jog over the road. One of them jogs toward us, not quite sure yet why we're here. He is brought up to speed pretty fast as I punch him in the jaw with the brass knuckle and knock him out cold.

That rallies his colleagues into action and amidst some hollering and whistling, the remaining seven men come running toward us.

"Here we go," Mikey flashes his eyebrows at me and we run toward them. I punch the biggest one in the stomach as he reaches me and he drops to his knees before I punch him in the face and his nose busts open. The rest of the men surround us, but Mikey and I have faced much tougher odds and much tougher men than these before, and we make short work of them in less than ten minutes. They lie on the floor around us, groaning and clutching their broken limbs and faces and I stare down at them.

It was a simple brawl. That was all I came for and it released some of the pent up tension I've been feeling these past few weeks. I look around for Mikey, who has one of the men on the floor. He straddles his chest and rains blows down on him. I watch for a few seconds and when he doesn't show any signs of letting up, I jog over to him and put my hand on his shoulder. He doesn't stop though. I'm not sure he even knows I'm standing right here.

The guy on the floor no longer even has a face and is most definitely dead, but it doesn't stop my younger brother laying into him like he's fighting for his life.

"Mikey! Come on, son. We need to get out of here."

He turns and looks at me, blood spattered over his face and a look in his eyes that I haven't seen for a very long time. I grab his arm and pull him up, just as one of the men from the floor stumbles over and looks at his dead workmate in horror. I grab him by the throat and squeeze. "You know who we are?" I snarl at him.

He nods, his eyes wide with fear.

"You tell anyone who or what you saw here tonight and I will hunt you and every single member of your family down. You understand me?"

"Yes, Mr Ryan."

"This is the end of it. Right here. Right now!" I hiss at him and he nods his agreement.

I drag Mikey to the car and we jump inside before I drive us away from the place as fast as the jeep will take us.

"I saw him, Shane," Mikey says as he stares at me. "I was punching that guy but I saw his face."

"Who?"

"Patrick Ryan!" he spits the name out as though it leaves a bitter taste in his mouth.

"You feel better?" I ask him.

"Yeah," he nods.

"Good. And I doubt they'll be giving any of our bouncers any more shit. So, mission accomplished!"

Mikey leans back in his seat and closes his eyes and I drive us back to our apartment.

CHAPTER 34

JESSIE

*I*t's our last night on the road as we'll be home tomorrow evening and I such have a mixture of feelings about the whole thing. I'm excited to see Liam and Mikey. A little sad to end my time alone with Conor. And nervous as hell to see Shane. Despite what Conor tries to assure me, I don't think our differences can be fixed with a simple conversation.

I walk across the parking lot toward the motel as Conor takes his bag from the trunk. The lot is almost empty except for a light blue pick-up a few yards away from me. I barely notice it, until the driver starts the engine and it sputters to life. Glancing over at it as the driver pulls out of his space and turns the vehicle, I get a glimpse of him. He looks directly at me and my legs nearly buckle beneath me. My blood freezes in my veins as time seems to stand still. I have seen those eyes before. I'm sure I have.

My body moves entirely on instinct. I turn and run in the opposite direction, straight into Conor's arms. He places his hands on my shoulders as I struggle to run past him. Has he brought me here to hand me over, after all? Was Alexei telling the truth about the Ryan brothers?

My heart pounds in my chest. Blood thunders in my ears and

tears run down my face. I have to get out of here. I try to wrench my arms from Conor's grip so I can run, but he holds me tight to him. He is speaking but I can't hear him because my senses are completely overloaded. My feet stumble on the asphalt and I'm falling. I can't breathe. I gasp in a mouthful of air, but it doesn't quite reach my lungs. I'm going to pass out. Right here. And he's going to take me. The Wolf is going to take me away.

"Jessie!" Conor shouts loudly, penetrating the fog of confusion I'm enveloped in.

I blink up at him as he stares down at me, his dark brown eyes full of concern. "What's going on?" he asks, his voice softer as one of his hands slides through my hair until it rests against the back of my neck. "Talk to me, Angel."

"Volk," I whisper, reverting to the name he made me use for him. Russian for Wolf. "He's here."

Conor looks around the parking lot. "There's no-one here but us," he frowns as he looks down at me.

"The blue pick-up," I mumble as I lean my face against his chest.

"The one that just drove out of here?"

"It was him, Conor."

He takes a sharp intake of breath and the muscles in his chest and arms tense and flex. "Let's get into the motel, Angel," he says softly.

I turn my head, my eyes darting around the now empty car lot to make sure he's really gone before I allow Conor to walk me toward the motel with one of his huge arms wrapped around me. My legs continue to tremble and my heart is still hammering against my ribcage, but I can see and hear clearly now. I wipe the tears from my eyes with the back of my hand. Conor is on high alert too, checking all around us as we make our way to our motel room.

As soon as we're inside, he bolts the door behind us and pulls his Glock from his bag, tucking it into the waistband of his jeans. "You want me to go check outside?" he asks.

I shake my head. "No. Stay in here with me."

"Okay," he whispers as he pulls me back to him, wrapping his arms around me and pressing a kiss on the top of my head. "Tell me what you saw, Angel."

I suck in a shaky breath. "That guy in the pick-up. He looked straight at me. And his eyes. I would never forget those eyes." I shudder.

"You're sure it was him?" he asks as he smooths my hair with one hand.

I close my eyes and picture his face again. He looked right at me. Did he smile at me like he knew me too? Did he even look like the Wolf? Here in the safety of Conor's arms, I'm not sure at all. "I don't know," I sniff. "He was far away. He didn't look exactly like him. He was clean shaven. I never saw the Wolf without a beard. But he had those same grey eyes."

Conor looks down at me, cupping my chin in his hand. "How would he know we were here, though? We didn't even know we'd be here until about thirty minutes ago."

"I know. I just saw him... and I..." I shake my head and press my face back against his chest. I feel like such an idiot. I have been preparing to face that man down for the past eight years, but the minute I see someone who looks like him, I have a full on panic attack.

"You're safe now, Angel," he whispers against my ear. "I will never let anyone hurt you. I promise."

"Can we just stay in here for rest of the night?"

"Sure. I'll order us some takeout and we can veg in front of the TV. Okay?"

I nod, my face brushing against his shirt as I wrap my arms around his waist and out of nowhere tears start running down my cheeks. I suck in a deep breath as I try to stop sobbing, but it only makes me worse and I let out a strangled, choking noise that causes Conor's whole body to tense as he squeezes me tighter to him. "Jessie," he says softly and the concern in his voice only makes me cry more.

WHEN I'VE FINALLY STOPPED CRYING and shaking, Conor and I sit at the small table in the motel room. I pick at my fingernails while he stares at me and I feel concern and anger coming from him in waves. I look down at my hands, avoiding his gaze because I can't bear to see the hurt in them.

"You want to talk about it, Angel?" he asks softly.

"I don't know. I've never told anyone about what he did." I shudder and Conor reaches for me and takes hold of my hand, brushing his fingertips over my palm and soothing my frayed edges the way that only he can.

"Maybe it will help?"

I look up at his face and stare into his deep brown eyes, which are so full of love and concern that it makes me feel completely safe and protected. "After he murdered my family… the Wolf, he tied me up with duct tape. He put some over my mouth too, and then he put me in the trunk of his car and we must have driven for almost a day before he stopped and let me out. We were at his house in the mountains. It was so dark, like pitch black. There were no streetlights or anything. I couldn't see a thing as he made me walk to the house."

I swallow hard as my heart begins to race again and Conor squeezes my hand gently. "It's okay, Angel. We got all night."

I give him a faint smile before I continue speaking. "That first night, he took me to a room and he…" I choke down a sob as I recall the first time he raped me. "I tried to fight him. I kicked and scratched and I screamed so loudly that I felt like my throat was bleeding, but he just laughed at me." I feel the tear running down my cheek and Conor brushes it away with his free hand. "I'd never even kissed a boy before. It hurt so bad, like nothing I'd ever experienced. I thought I was going to die. But even worse than the pain was the smell of him. He stunk of cigarettes and stale sweat, and it was suffocating. *He* was suffocating. His pale, clammy skin against mine. I closed my eyes and tried to block it all out. My mom was big into meditation and she taught me how to tune out the world, but I couldn't escape the smell of him, no matter what I did." I draw in a shaky breath and realize tears are running down my cheeks again.

"Jessie," Conor whispers as his eyes search my face and I see the anger and the pain I'm causing him. It's the same kind of hurt I experience when I think about what Conor and his brothers endured as children. It is the same pain I feel when I think about my parents and my innocent little brothers and the night they were slaughtered in front of my eyes. I know that it doesn't come from a place of pity or sympathy, but from pure love.

"After that night, he would come to my room most nights. And when he started to trust me a little more, he would summon me to his. The house was a fortress. I knew I could have over-ridden the security systems, but I was always locked in my room or his, and when I wasn't, he was always watching me. I swear he hardly slept. I tried to escape almost every day for the first few weeks I was there, but he always caught me and punished me and I realized I would have to play the long game. And that was when I started to pay attention to what he liked and what made him lose control. Even at sixteen, I understood that when he'd just got off was when he was at his most vulnerable. He used to tie me up for sex most of the time. Duct tape was a favorite of his, but after he began to trust me, he would untie me after. I think he even believed that I was beginning to develop feelings for him."

I brush the tears from my eyes and smile at Conor who still watches me intently. That actually did make me feel better. Saying those things out loud made them seem less powerful. They are memories now. They do not define me. The Wolf and what he did to me will not define who I am.

Conor leans forward and takes both of my hands in his. "You are a goddamn warrior, Jessie. And when we find the Wolf, we will make him pay, Angel. I promise I would die before I let him ever touch you again."

I lift his hand to my face and press a soft kiss on his knuckles. "You'd better not die, Conor Ryan! Not ever."

"Well, I'll certainly do my best, Angel," he smiles at me.

TWO HOURS LATER, I'm lying on the bed with Conor's Glock beside me while he takes a shower. I still feel jumpy and anxious, but at least I can breathe now. We ate our takeout an hour ago, and I finally relaxed enough for him to consider leaving me alone for five minutes to take a shower.

I'm watching *Fast and Furious,* and although this is one of my favorite films, I am barely concentrating on it. When Conor walks back into the room a moment later, with a towel wrapped around his waist, some of the tension slips away from me again. Being around him makes me feel so much better. I feel completely safe when I'm with him, and I wasn't sure I would ever experience that feeling ever again.

He dries himself off and pulls on a pair of shorts before lying on the bed beside me. He holds out his arm and I snuggle against his muscular chest, taking comfort from his warm skin against mine and the sound of his heartbeat against my ear.

"You okay, Angel?" he whispers as he pushes my hair back from my face.

"I am now."

CHAPTER 35

CONOR

I glance down at Jessie, fast asleep in my arms, and kiss the top of her head before moving her carefully off me. The panic and the terror in her face earlier scared the living shit out of me. This girl has balls of fucking steel. I have never seen her scared like that before, not even when I stuck a semi-automatic in her face that first day I met her. Not when those assholes tried to drag her into their truck the day before, or when we drugged her and kidnapped her. But today, she was genuinely, bone shaking terrified.

Sliding out of bed, I take my cell phone off the nightstand and walk to the bathroom to make a call so I don't wake her.

Shane answers the phone on the second ring. "Hey. What's up?"

"You answered that fast," I say, glancing at my watch and seeing it's almost 2am, but then my overprotective big brother rarely sleeps, and he sleeps even less when Jessie isn't in his bed.

"I saw your name and wondered why you're calling me at this hour of night."

"Yeah, well. Something happened today, bro."

"What now?" he asks, the edge audible in his voice.

"Jessie thought she saw the Wolf."

"What? Where?"

"In a pickup in the parking lot of our motel. But he drove away and I've checked the lot a dozen times since and he hasn't come back. I'm not sure it was him. I mean, how could he know we were here? And it's some coincidence for her to just run into him otherwise."

"Did you get a look at him? Did he seem like he recognized her?"

"I didn't see anything. By the time she'd told me, the guy was long gone."

"You think it was him?"

"I don't know. But, fuck Shane, I have never seen our girl act like that before. She almost ran straight through me trying to get away. It was like she couldn't even see me. I thought she was going to fucking pass out from terror."

"Is she okay?" he asks, the concern in his voice clear to hear and I wish that she could realize just how much he cares for her.

"Yeah, she is now. She's sleeping. You really got nothing on this Wolf guy yet? Or where he might be?"

"No. And if Jessie and Alexei have been looking for him for the past eight years and never come close to finding him, I don't hold out much hope that I will. Not without Jessie's help anyway. When will you be home?"

"Tomorrow night."

"Good. The sooner we have you both back here, the better," he says with a sigh.

"You okay?" I ask him. He carries so much responsibility on his shoulders and I wish he would share more of it with me and our younger brothers. We're not little kids anymore. He doesn't have to protect us all from everything. I poke my head out of the door to check on Jessie and smile when I see she hasn't moved from the position I left her in. She makes Shane more relaxed and much less tense, and I need to get her home to him as soon as I can.

"Yeah," he replies. "Just dealing with some shit from back home."

"That old cunt not dead yet?" I snarl.

"Nope."

"Good. Dying is too good for that fucker."

"I know. Erin told me he doesn't have long left though."

"Erin's been there a lot lately."

"What the fuck does that mean, Conor?" he snaps.

"Just an observation. I'd hate for you to get sucked into any of her shit, that's all. That woman is fucking dangerous."

"I'm pretty sure I can handle her. Besides, she's just dealing with some paperwork for me. That deal I told you about back in Ireland is almost done."

"Good," I nod my head. He's about to make us a fortune selling some old family property.

"Look after her, Conor. And if she sees that guy again, or you sense anything untoward going on, call me and we'll come meet you both."

"I will. Thanks. But I'm sure everything is going to be fine, and we'll see you tomorrow night."

After I finish the call to Shane, I slip back into bed and Jessie stirs beside me. "Where have you been?" she whispers as she cuddles back into me.

"I just called Shane."

"Why?" She sits up. Is something wrong?"

"No." I reach out and tuck her hair behind her ear. "I wanted to tell him what happened today, that's all. Just in case he'd heard anything about the Wolf being active again."

"And has he?"

"No. He would have told me if he had. I just wanted to speak to him, I suppose. I was worried about you."

She lies down again, resting her head on her elbow. "I have to tell you something, Conor," she whispers and my heart constricts in my chest.

"What, Angel?"

"When I saw him today, or thought I saw him, I thought about what Alexei said to me. About you and your brothers wanting to hand me over to him…" She chokes back a sob and doesn't finish the sentence.

That fucking hurts. But, I suppose I can't blame her. I don't think anyone in Jessie's life has ever been completely straight with her. Even her parents lied to her, and although I completely get their reasons why, I guess that leaves a mark. I have always had my brothers, and their honesty and respect means the world to me. Jessie didn't have that for so long, I guess she's forgotten what it feels like to know without a doubt that someone will always have your back, no matter what.

I turn on my side so I'm facing her and brush the back of my knuckles over her cheek. "What is it going to take for you to trust me, Angel?"

"I do trust you, Conor. It was just for a second. I was terrified. I know you would never hurt me," she whispers.

I roll on top of her, taking hold of her wrists and pinning them to the side of her head. "You do?"

"Yes," she breathes.

"Then show me, Angel."

"How?"

I release her hands and reach down to the edge of her tank top, pulling it up her body, I stop when I reach her neck and pull her arms out. Then I roll it up over her face until it rests over her eyes. "Don't move," I whisper in her ear, and her body shivers beneath me. Pushing myself up from the bed, I go to my bag and take out the duct tape I always carry. It comes in handy in my profession when you never know when you might need to tie someone up and throw them in the trunk of your car.

I pull the end of the tape and the distinctive sound makes her flinch slightly. "What's that?" she breathes.

"You know what it is, Angel."

"What are you going to do with it?"

I kneel on the bed and take hold of her hands, pulling them down by her sides. "What do you think?"

She bites on her lower lip in that adorable way that makes me want to eat her alive, but she doesn't ask me to stop. Maybe this is a shitty thing to do after what she told me the Wolf did to her, but I can't think of a more effective or quicker way to prove to her she can trust me.

I peel off some tape and tear off a huge strip with my teeth. "Bring your knees up, Angel. I want you to hold your ankles," I instruct and she does so without question. Her body trembles as I tape her left wrist to her left ankle. Her breathing gets heavier and I can see her breasts rising and falling with each deep breath she takes. Tearing off some more tape, I do the same to her right side, until she is bound tight and unable to move her limbs. I get off the bed again and walk back to my bag.

"Conor," she whispers.

"I'm right here," I tell her as I take the large knife from the zip inside my bag and walk back toward her. Climbing onto the bed, I kneel between her spread thighs. "I forgot to take off your panties, Angel."

"I know."

I place the tip of the blade between her breasts and she shudders as I run it down over her stomach. As the blade gets lower, she writhes beneath it.

"Conor!" She groans my name this time, and the sound makes my cock throb.

"You look beautiful lying here spread open and bound for me," I growl as I slide the edge of the knife beneath the band of her underwear. "Don't move, Angel," I remind her as I take hold of her panties with my free hand and slice through the band of cotton at either side, near her hipbones, until they fall apart and expose her beautiful pink pussy to me. Dipping my finger inside her, I stifle a groan as I find her wet for me. "Dammit, Jessie. You're soaking already."

Her thighs tremble as I pump my finger in and out of her pussy and she moans softly for me as I add a second. I put the knife on the nightstand and run my hand up the inside of her thigh, rubbing two fingers over her swollen clit while I keep finger fucking her with my other hand. She gets wetter with each passing second, soaking my fingers with her cum until the sound of her wet heat is echoing around the room and I am so fucking hard, I feel like I could come just from touching her.

"You love my fingers inside you, don't you, Angel?" I growl.

"Yes," she pants.

"You want more?" I add a third finger before she can even reply, stretching her wide for me, and her hips almost shoot off the bed.

"I love you, Conor," she moans loudly, and it completely undoes me. I slide my fingers out of her pussy and lie between her thighs, pressing my cock against her slick entrance.

"I love you too, Angel," I breathe before sealing my mouth over hers as I drive my cock deep inside her. I swallow her moans with my own as I fuck us both to the release we need. She shudders beneath me when she comes, her entire body moving because her limbs are pinned to it. I look at her, completely at my mercy and completely mine, and feel like my heart might burst out of my chest. I love this woman so much it fucking hurts.

"Conor," she whimpers when I let her up for air. I pull her tank top from her eyes and over her head so she can see again.

"Hey, you," I smile at her.

"Hey," she breathes.

"You okay?"

"Yes," she smiles back at me.

"You want me to untie you, Angel?"

"Yes, please."

I place a soft kiss on her lips as I pull my cock out of her and grab my knife again. Then I move down the bed, planting a kiss on her pussy before I cut through the tape on her wrists and ankles.

"Ow," she says as I gently peel off the first piece. "I knew I'd get you to punish me eventually," she giggles.

"Jessie!" I warn her as I nip her inner thigh. "This isn't a punishment, Angel. This is me not thinking through my plan thoroughly enough. I forgot how hard this stuff is to get off. I don't usually have to be so considerate when I'm removing it."

"Just pull it off quickly, Conor," she groans. "It's like ripping a band aid. The slower you do it, the more it hurts."

I pull her skin taut and pull the tape quickly and she winces. Rubbing the reddened skin, I look up at her, but she is smiling at me. I do the same to her other side and she stretches her limbs when she is free.

I move back up the bed toward her and pull her into my arms.

"Why do you have duct tape in your bag, Conor? Were you planning on kidnapping me if I didn't come with you voluntarily?" she asks with a grin.

I suck on my lip, as though I'm deep in thought and she pushes me playfully on the chest. "I was never intending to use it on you, Angel. But if you'd refused to come with me, I might have tied you up with your own panties and driven you back to New York."

"My panties?" She raises one eyebrow at me.

"Yes."

"So, the duct tape?"

"You'd be surprised by how often it comes in useful," I shrug.

"And not just duct tape. Did you cut off my panties with a knife, Conor Ryan?"

"I did," I grin at her.

"You're a devil," she laughs and the sound makes me so fucking happy.

"I never pretended to be anything else, Angel."

"So, did I prove how much I trust you then?" she asks from beneath her long lashes as she looks down.

I cup her chin and tilt her face so I can look into those incredible blue eyes. "Yes," I reply and then I press my lips against hers and kiss her and she melts into me, her fingers curling in my hair as she presses her hot body against mine. As she lifts her leg and hooks it over mine to pull me even closer to her, I slide my hand to her ass and think I might just be the happiest man in the whole fucking world.

CHAPTER 36

SHANE

*A*fter speaking to Conor last night, I lay awake until the early hours of the morning, thinking about him and Jessie out there on the road alone. Jessie believing she saw the Wolf must have terrified her, and I hate to admit it, but it's freaked me out too. There is so little we know about him, it makes me nervous. He literally just upped and disappeared eight years ago. If he is still alive, he could be anyone. Jessie is the only person known to have seen his face and lived to tell the tale. If she thinks she saw him yesterday, who are we to say she was mistaken? Although Conor seems to think she was, and I suppose I'll have to trust his gut.

Rubbing my temples, I wince at the pain as it sears through my forehead. I think I fell asleep at four and was awake again by seven. I need to get some decent fucking sleep. I've always been a bit of an insomniac, but the truth is I've never slept as well as I did when Jessie was here. Even when she wasn't in my bed, just knowing she was close by helped. And when she was in my bed — well, I slept like a fucking baby. The sooner Conor gets her back home safely to us, the better for everyone.

My cell phone vibrates on the table in front of me, and I

glance at the screen. It's an unknown number. I accept the call and hold the phone to my ear, but I don't speak.

"That you, boy?" I hear a voice on the other end of the line that sounds vaguely familiar. The accent is hard to place, no doubt a result of living in so many countries and never settling in one long enough to call it home, but there is a distinct Irish lilt buried in that low, gravelly tone that is probably only detectable to someone who grew up around it.

"Paul?"

"Who else?"

"What the fuck? I haven't seen you for almost twenty-five years. Where the hell have you been?"

"Around. You know I had to get out of there, Shane."

"Yeah? Well, we all did," I say with a sigh as I rub a hand over my jaw as the memories of my Uncle Paul teaching me to shoot a sniper rifle when I was ten years old come rushing to the surface of my brain. I had almost forgotten about it. He was a marksman in the army and he was never around that much, but whenever he came home from tour, he always stayed with us. They were some of the happiest memories of my childhood. But just like he ruined everything else, my father eventually drove Paul away. He left when I was fourteen and the last I heard, he was working as a mercenary for some very bad people in Italy. I assumed he was dead.

"I hear the evil old fucker is dying?" he says before he's overcome with a fit of coughing.

"Yeah. You don't sound very well yourself, Uncle? Everything okay?"

"Me? I'm fucking invincible, nephew. Don't you remember?" he laughs, but it's a cold one, because there is nothing amusing about what he just said. My father almost killed him at least half a dozen times.

"Is that why you've resurfaced? You think he's left you something in his will?"

He laughs out loud at that — a genuine one this time. "I wouldn't accept a penny of that sadistic fuck's money! But I'll go to his funeral, if only to make sure he's really dead. And then I'll piss on his grave."

"You spoken to him at all these last few years?"

"No!" he snarls. "Have you?"

"No. I haven't seen or spoken to him since we came to New York."

"Ten years!" Paul lets out a low whistle. "A long time not to see your father, Shane!" he sneers.

"How did you even know we left Ireland?" I frown as I turn on my computer. He knows we left ten years ago, and that makes me nervous.

"I've kept tabs on my nephews. Condolences on your failed engagement, by the way," he chuckles.

"Fuck you!"

"Still got that smart mouth, I see. So, why did you finally leave?"

"It's a long fucking story."

"Well, then you can tell me at the old fucker's funeral?"

"Maybe," I sigh. "Where the fuck have you been, Pol?"

"I told you. Around."

"You still killing people for a living?"

"Shane," he feigns his indignation. "We never discuss business on the phone."

"No, of course not," I laugh. "But, now that we are. In your line of work, you ever come across the Wolf?"

He doesn't reply, and I listen to the sound of his labored breathing for a few seconds. "Why the fuck are you interested in the Wolf, kid?" he eventually snaps.

"Professional curiosity."

"I hear he retired, but there's a rumor he's resurfaced."

My heart seems like it stops beating, as though Paul has just thrust his hand into my chest and has it squeezed in his fist. "You have any idea where he is?" I grind out the words.

"Russia, or so I heard. Why the hell do you need to know anything about the Wolf?" he asks again.

"Nothing really. I told you, professional curiosity."

"You don't need the services of a hitman, Shane. Between me and your father, didn't we teach you enough about how to deal with your enemies by yourself, kid?"

"You sure fucking did," I snap. Pair of sadistic assholes.

"Yeah? Well, stay away from the Wolf. He's bad news."

"Isn't everyone? Anyway, you said he's in Russia. So he's nowhere near New York, is he?"

"You hiding something from me, kid?"

"Plenty. But not about this, no," I lie again. "So, I'll be seeing you soon then, Uncle?"

"It seems so," he coughs again. "Let's hope that cunt dies soon, eh?"

"Hmm," I agree, but my mind is elsewhere. Where the hell has Paul been all these years?

After I end the call, I open one of Jessie's files on my computer. I make a quick scan of the document, which comprises bank details and money transfers dating back at least ten years. I have no clue what I'm looking for, but I'm hoping something might jump out at me. Because I am no closer to finding out where Alexei Ivanov is, and I know he holds me and my brothers responsible for losing his daughter — again. It's only a matter of time before he comes looking for vengeance. And when he does, he will most definitely find it, because I have made it my mission in life to kill that psychopathic motherfucker for everything he has put Jessie and my brothers through.

Once he gets a sniff that she is back with us, he will act quickly to get her back. So, we need to strike first. But it's hard to do that when we have no idea where the slippery Russian prick is, whereas we are right where he knows to find us. However, I'll be fucked if I'll run and hide from him or anyone else. The Ryan brothers hide from no-one.

A FEW MINUTES LATER, I turn off my computer again. My conversation with my uncle is playing on my mind. Something is niggling in the back of my mind like an itch that I can't quite reach to scratch. So, the Wolf is back? Why now? Has Alexei's discovery of Jessie's survival reached him too somehow? Nobody knows who the Wolf is. He could be one of Alexei's own men, for all we know.

I close my eyes and rub my head again. This whole fucked up situation is making my headache even worse. And the best way I know to soothe any tension is currently a half day's drive away. But tonight she's going to be standing right here. And fuck, I might just tie her to my bed and bury myself so far inside her that we both forget about everything that's happened these past three months. Except that as much as I wish I could, I can't forget. I may even be able to forgive her one day, but I will never be able to trust her again.

"Hey, Erin is here." The sound of my younger brother Mikey's voice snaps me from my thoughts.

"What? Why?" I frown at him. I'm not expecting her.

Mikey shrugs. "I don't know, bro. But she's on her way up now."

"Fine," I sigh as I lean back in my chair.

"I can tell her you're in a meeting if you like?" he offers.

"No. It's fine," I say with a shake of my head. "She's been working on some contracts for me. She might have some news at last. Just tell her to come through."

"Will do," Mikey says with a nod of his head before he disappears out of the doorway again. Of all the days Erin decides to show up here, it has to be the day Jessie is coming home. I already have a ball of dread in my stomach at the thought of facing her after everything that's happened. Perhaps I'm fooling myself that Jessie coming back here has anything to do with me. I sent Conor after her, because I see the love she has for him. The connection they have runs deep. He never doubted her, even when I was sure she had betrayed us.

CHAPTER 37

JESSIE

*W*iping my hands on my napkin, I look across the table at Conor as he finishes his last mouthful of steak. I smile at him and he winks back at me.

"I have loved these past few days with you," I say.

He swallows his food and puts his knife and fork on his plate. "I've loved them too, Angel. I'm almost sad we're nearly home."

"Almost?" I arch an eyebrow at him.

"Being on the road with you and having you all to myself has been incredible, but I've been gone for two months. I've never been apart from my brothers for that long before."

"I'm sorry," I say as a wave of guilt washes over me.

"Don't be," he frowns as he places his large hand over mine. "I would do it all again in a heartbeat, and I would spend my entire life searching for you, Jessie."

"I'm glad you found me, Conor," I say before I begin to chew on my lip absent-mindedly.

"You nervous about going home, Angel?" he asks softly.

"I'm nervous about seeing him."

Conor nods, knowing that I'm talking about Shane. Of all of

them, it took him the longest to let me in. I know it cost him. And despite the promises I made to him, I left as soon as I had a single doubt. "I'm sure he's feeling the same," Conor says with a smile. "You two have a lot to talk about."

I take a deep breath. "Yeah."

"That's if Liam and Mikey don't steal you away as soon as you set foot back in the apartment," he laughs, and his brown eyes twinkle. The closer we have got to New York, the happier and more relaxed Conor has become. That I have kept him away from them all for so long weighs heavily on me, no matter what he says.

A FEW HOURS LATER, Conor presses me against the wall in the elevator in his New York apartment building and kisses me softly. "These last few days have been incredible, Jessie," he breathes when he breaks our kiss.

"I know."

"As soon as we get into the apartment, my brothers are going to want you all to themselves, and I need to get back to work in the club. But know that I will be thinking about you every second. I love you so fucking much, Angel."

"I love you too, Conor," I groan as he dips his head low and peppers soft kisses along my throat.

"Promise me we can take a road trip every once in a while. Just you and me."

"I promise."

The elevator stops and the doors slide open. I look up at him. "Thank you for coming to rescue me and bringing me home."

"Any time, Angel," he growls as he takes my hand and leads me out into the hallway. I see someone in my peripheral vision and I turn toward Shane's office to see him standing about twenty feet away from me. My heart races. I swallow hard as our eyes lock. I have been both dreading and looking forward to this moment. For what seems like an eternity, we just stand there staring at each other, neither of us speaking or making any movement. I'm aware of Conor standing beside me still, but my eyes remain locked on Shane. My pulse thrums against my wrists and my throat.

It seems as though he is about to speak, but he turns instead, distracted by the sound of a voice from behind him. Someone is coming from the direction of his office. My stomach drops to the floor when I see who it is.

Erin. His ex-fiancée. What the hell is she doing here? And on today of all days. He knew I was coming back today. Has he done this to deliberately hurt me? Or have I even featured in his plans at all?

He told me I would never be one of them. Perhaps, instead of fantasizing about him and me together, I should listen to what he actually said to me, and make my peace with the fact that Shane and I can never be what we once were.

Erin places a manicured hand on his shoulder and whispers something in his ear. His eyes flicker from mine and I take the opportunity to look away. The sound of the twins running down the hallway from the opposite direction makes me turn to them instead.

Mikey reaches me first. "Red!" he shouts as he picks me up and spins me around, kissing me all over my face just as Liam reaches us. As soon as Mikey sets me on my feet, Liam pulls me into his huge arms. "I've missed you, baby," he growls in my ear.

"I've missed you both too," I reply as I take a step back.

Conor coughs as if to remind us all he is standing there, and Mikey wraps an arm around his neck. "We've missed you too, bro," he laughs.

"Yeah, and everyone in the club has missed you too! You need to get your ass down there and sort some shit out," Liam adds as he wraps one arm around me and slaps Conor on the back with his free hand.

Conor raises his eyebrows at me. "I'd better be going, Angel. I'll see you tomorrow. Don't wear these boys out now."

"I won't," I smile at him. "Have a good night down there."

He laughs. "I'm sure it will be all kinds of fun," then he leans forward and kisses me softly on the cheek before he goes back to the elevator. I glance back down the hallway and notice that Shane and Erin are no longer there.

"You need food or something to drink?" Liam asks, and I drag my eyes back to his handsome face.

"No. Conor and I ate a few hours ago. I'm good."

"You want to watch a movie?" Mikey asks, his eyes narrowed as they roam over my body.

"Actually, I'm kind of tired," I say.

"Your bedroom is all ready for you, baby. Just how you left it," Liam whispers in my ear.

"Thank you," I say and a flush creeps over my chest and neck and suddenly I feel awkward and nervous.

Mikey steps toward me and presses his lips against my ear. "You mind if Liam and I join you, Red? Because ever since we watched Conor fucking you in that motel room, we've done nothing but think about tasting you again."

Liam's hand slides to my ass and he kisses the other side of my neck, making me drag in a deep breath as the heat rushes between my thighs and I experience the familiar fluttering in my abdomen. "Of course I don't mind. In fact, I was counting on it. I've missed you both too."

"Then let's get to bed and get you naked," Liam growls as he slaps my ass.

A FEW MINUTES LATER, the three of us are standing in my bedroom and I am sandwiched between their two hard bodies, with Mikey at my back and Liam at my front. Liam kisses me softly, his tongue swirling against mine as Mikey reaches in front of me and unzips my mini skirt before pushing it over my hips and down my legs. He runs his warm strong hands from my ankles, up the entire length of my legs as he stands upright again, until he reaches the edge of my tank top and he pulls that up and off over my head, forcing Liam and me to break our kiss for a second. When we do, Liam stares into my eyes and smiles at me while Mikey makes quick work of removing my bra and panties.

"I'm so fucking hard for you, Red," Mikey growls in my ear before he starts trailing kisses along the back of my neck.

Liam seals his mouth over mine again, one hand snaking around my hips and onto my ass and one slipping between my thighs until he reaches my slick folds. "She's dripping wet, bro," he says as he pulls back from me and I moan as he circles my clit with two fingers.

At the same time, Mikey's hand rubs over my ass from behind and then between my thighs. "Spread your legs wider, Red," he murmurs against my skin. "I want inside you."

I do as he says, and he slips two thick fingers into my pussy while Liam keeps on circling my clit and I groan out loud, making them both chuckle softly. They spend the next ten minutes kissing my lips, neck, back and breasts while they take turns finger fucking me, until my legs are trembling with my impending release.

"You want to come, baby?" Liam growls.

"Yes. Please," I pant as they double their efforts and their bodies press closer against me until they are the only things holding me up as my orgasm tears through me like black powder. When they have rubbed the last of my climax from me, Liam lifts me and carries me over to the bed while Mikey undresses. Pressing my thighs flat to the bed, he leans down and licks the length of my pussy. "Fuck, you taste even better than I remember,

Jessie," he groans before he sucks my clit into his warm mouth and my hips almost jolt off the bed in pleasure.

As soon as Mikey is undressed, he climbs onto the bed too, crawling up toward my face and pressing his lips over mine. His tongue pushes inside my mouth at the same time Liam's pushes into my opening and he begins toying with my pebbled nipples. I whimper as the two of them bring me to the edge again. They work my body together so expertly, as though they always know what the other one is thinking.

Suddenly, I no longer feel Liam's mouth between my thighs. "You need to taste this sweet pussy, Mikey," he says with a chuckle.

"I thought you'd never ask," Mikey grins as he plants a final kiss on my lips and disappears, to be replaced by his twin. Liam kisses me, swirling his tongue against mine so that I can taste myself on him and the wet heat floods my pussy. Mikey growls in appreciation as he laps at my opening. A few moments later, the two of them bring me to another earth shattering climax. I try to scream their names but Liam swallows the sounds as he keeps his mouth sealed over mine.

When the last of my orgasm has rolled through my body, Liam lets me up for air. "Turn on your side, baby," he growls as Mikey moves back up the bed. "Facing me."

I shuffle onto my side and Mikey slides in behind me. "Neither of us can wait a minute longer to fuck you, Red," he whispers against my ear. "So we're both going to. You okay with that?"

"You know I am," I breathe as Liam rolls over and pulls a tube of lube from the nightstand before tossing it to his brother. He cups my chin in his hand as Mikey snaps the cap and I can feel him coating his cock directly behind me.

"You are so fucking beautiful, Jessie," Liam whispers. "I can't wait to feel you come on my cock, baby. I've missed you so fucking much."

I reach out and stroke his cheek with my hand as I blink back tears. "I've missed you too," I whisper.

Mikey rolls back into me, his slick cock nudging at the seam of my ass as he lifts my thigh into the air. "But, if you ever run away from us again, Red, we won't be so forgiving. You belong here with us. So don't even think about abandoning us for a third time," he warns and a thrill of pleasure shoots through me at his possessiveness.

"Hmm. You got that, baby?" Liam adds as he slides his cock deep inside me until the waves of pleasure roll over my body.

"Uh-huh," I groan.

"You ready for me too now?" Mikey asks as he plants a soft kiss on my shoulder blade.

"Yes," I breathe and he edges the tip of his cock inside me too.

"Did Conor fuck this beautiful ass the other night? Is that what he didn't want us to watch?"

"Yes," I groan as he pushes in deeper while Liam's cock twitches inside me.

"I think Mikey better hurry," Liam chuckles as my walls squeeze around him. "Because I feel you on the edge already, baby. Hold on a little longer."

"I'm trying," I pant. "But you're not making it easy."

"Then you'd better help me out, bro," Mikey laughs softly as he lifts my leg higher into the air while Liam slides his hand to my ass and spreads me open to allow his brother easier access.

"Relax, Red, you know you can take me," Mikey soothes in my ear as he pushes in deeper until he is all the way inside. I groan loudly at the sensation of being so completely full of them while I'm pressed between their hard, hot bodies. "Fuck, Jessie! You're going to make me come in about two minutes, because this ass is so freaking hot and tight," he growls.

I groan loudly as they both fuck me in a perfect rhythm. Each of them seeming to be aware of exactly what the other is doing and knowing precisely where to touch and kiss me to keep me teetering on the edge of oblivion. I am sandwiched tightly between them as they kiss and touch and fuck every part of me with such desire and tenderness that I start to see stars flickering behind my eyelids.

I have missed these two so much and I wonder how I was ever crazy enough to leave any of them. This is exactly where I belong. This is home, and I will never leave again.

CHAPTER 38

SHANE

The whiskey burns my throat as I swallow two shots' worth in one large gulp before I slam the glass down on my desk. Jessie is back. I thought that I could handle seeing her and not want to punish her, or fuck her, but as soon as I saw her I wanted to do both.

Fortunately, I didn't get the chance to do either because as soon as she saw them she fell into the arms of my younger brothers instead.

I don't begrudge them their happiness with her. They have missed her like crazy, and learning of our father's impending demise has dredged up all kinds of shit from their pasts for them. So, why is there a ball of anger searing a hole in my chest? It burns white hot as I recall the way she looked at me. I have so much that I want to say to her, but she's made it clear that she hasn't come back for me. And how can I blame her after what I did the last time she was here? I suppose that's only a good thing because I can't go back there with her. It would kill me to lose her again.

"You want another?" Erin's voice purrs from beside me.

"Yeah," I snap and she pours me another large measure of

Jameson's and a small one for herself. She suggested a drink to celebrate the deal we closed today, and after my brief encounter with Jessie, it seemed like a good idea. But, it's not.

As I look up at Erin, her cheeks flushed pink from the alcohol and her eyelashes fluttering, I realize it's a very bad idea. Erin has repeatedly made her feelings for me more than clear. She would jump at the chance for us to get back together, even though I've never given her any indication that I'm interested in reconciling. Apart from that one time, shortly after we'd called off the wedding, when we were both lonely and she'd turned up here in tears. But I swore to her and myself we would never do that again.

"Here you go." She hands me the glass and her fingers brush mine as I take it from her. She smiles at me, looking up through her long dark lashes and I'm suddenly reminded of the night we first met back in Ireland almost fifteen years ago.

We were at an event for the law firm she was working for. I remember thinking she was the most beautiful woman in the room. She'd been there with her fiancé that night, but she had left with me, and we had stayed together for the next ten years. Coming to New York had always been a dream of hers, and when all that shit went down with my father and the twins, it had seemed like the perfect time to move.

We'd had our whole future mapped out — or at least I'd thought we had. But Erin had an entirely different future in mind. One that included babies and a house in the suburbs, and that just isn't the life for me.

"For someone who just made a few million dollars this afternoon, you seem pretty miserable, Shane," Erin says, snapping me from my thoughts.

I shake my head. "Sorry," I mumble before I down the second glass of whiskey.

"Will you slow down? I'm struggling to keep up with you," she laughs softly as she downs her own drink.

"You don't have to keep up with me. In fact, you shouldn't." I arch an eyebrow at her. "You never could handle your liquor."

"Well, that was the old me. The new me is much tougher," she purrs as she perches on the edge of my desk and leans toward me.

"Is that so?"

"Yes," she replies as she holds out her glass until I grab hold of the bottle and pour us each another.

CHAPTER 39

CONOR

*A*s soon as the last of my bouncers leaves the club after closing time, I make my way through the basement of our building toward the elevator leading to our apartment. I would love nothing more than to crawl into bed with Jessie and press myself against her soft, warm body, but I know she'll be with the twins or Shane. I suppose I could do with some sleep anyway.

Just before I reach the elevator, I see Shane stepping out of the shadows and making his way toward me. "You up early, bro, or you not been to bed yet?" I smile as he reaches me. We caught up over a few shots of whiskey in my office just before midnight last night, but it wasn't enough. I have missed all of my brothers so fucking much.

"Both!" he grins at me. "I have a present for you," he says, indicating his head toward the other end of the basement.

"A present? For me?" I arch an eyebrow. "You shouldn't have."

"You won't be saying that when you see what it is," he chuckles softly as he starts walking away from me and toward the rooms we sometimes use down here for various purposes. Mostly to get information from our enemies. I experience a wave of guilt as I recall how we used one of these rooms to keep Jessie prisoner for a few days two months earlier.

I follow Shane until he stops at the door to my favorite room, containing all of my favorite toys and instruments, and I wonder what just what this present is he's referring to. He pulls out a huge key and unlocks the door before stepping inside with me close behind. There are two men, naked and strung up by their ankles, like two pig carcasses in a slaughterhouse.

At the sound of us coming into the room, they start to sputter and shake on their hooks. I can see they don't have tape on their mouths, although I see blood pouring down their faces and dripping onto the floor.

I look over at Shane as I close the door behind us. "Why do they sound funny?"

"I cut out their tongues," he says with a shrug.

I nod at him and then look back to the two men, wondering what they've done to incur my brother's wrath. It's not often he indulges in such depravity these days.

"You recognize them, Con?"

I step closer to them. Crouching down on my heels, I grab hold of one of them by his hair and lift his head slightly. It's hard to see his features fully in the dim room and through all of the blood and snot, but I smile when I realize who these two assholes are, and cutting out their tongues is going to be the least of their problems by the time I'm through with them.

The one who I'm holding onto squirms in my grip. A strangled gurgle comes out of his mouth and his eyes widen with fear as he recognizes me too.

"You remember what I said I'd do to you?" I say to him and he flinches. "You're going to wish I'd killed you in that parking lot while my girl watched, because she would have made me end it quickly. She's good like that. But now there's just me and my brother. And I am going to make you feel pain like you cannot even imagine," I snarl, and the second man wriggles and screams too, but the noise is drowned out by the sound of him choking on his own blood as it runs down his throat.

I stand tall and start to take off my jacket and shirt. I don't want them soaked in the blood of this pair of assholes.

"You certainly found these two and got them back here fast, Shane," I say as I unbutton my shirt. "I'm impressed."

"Impressed? Really? You underestimate me, bro," he grins at me as he unbuttons his shirt too.

"You joining me?"

"They put their hands on Jessie, didn't they?" he frowns.

"Yeah."

"You said they were going to kidnap and rape her?"

"Yup," I nod. "And this one," I kick one in the head and he howls in pain. "Said he was going to tear her apart."

"Then of course I'm fucking joining you," he says as he pulls his shirt off.

"Good," I smile at him. "It's been a while since we did this. I hope you remember what to do?"

"Don't forget who taught you everything you know, son," he frowns at me and I laugh out loud. I hated not being able to deal with these two fuckers back in Oklahoma, but now I'm fucking glad Jessie made me leave. Because making them pay for what they did to our girl is going to be so much more fun with Shane by my side.

It only takes two hours for us to torture John and Jeff to death. We could have made it last longer, but I need some sleep before I have to go back to work in a few hours. We walk through the basement, still shirtless and covered in blood.

"Is Jessie up yet?" I ask. "Because if she sees us like this… well, I don't have the energy to explain what we just did, bro."

"I have no idea," he shrugs.

"You haven't spoken to her yet?" I frown at him.

"No," he shakes his head. "She went off with the twins as soon as she got home."

"But you could have gone and spoken to her," I remind him. "It's not like you've never seen them all fucking before."

"Drop it, Con," he snaps.

"Drop it?" I snap back. "You've been waiting to speak to her for two months and now you're avoiding her?"

"I'm not avoiding her. It's complicated." He looks away from me. "My relationship with Jessie isn't as easy as yours."

"Well, you didn't exactly help matters having Erin here the day Jessie got back," I remind him.

"I couldn't help that. She finalized the Ireland deal for us and she needed me to sign some papers." He shakes his head. "Anyway, you should be fucking thanking me for what I just did, not giving me earache."

I wrap my arm around his neck. "I'm not giving you earache. But you and Jessie need to sort your shit out, bro. The whole fucking equilibrium is off when you two aren't right."

He nods his head, but I'm not sure he's convinced. He can't forgive Jessie for leaving us. He can't forgive himself for the way he treated her the last time she was here. So, he assumes that she won't forgive him either. I know that she already has, but I wish he would wake up and see how much she loves him, and how much he needs her.

CHAPTER 40

JESSIE

I sit at the breakfast table and smile across at Mikey sitting opposite me as we each eat a bowl of Lucky Charms.

"I've missed you, Red," he says as he swallows a mouthful of cereal.

"I've missed you too."

We both look up as Liam strolls into the room. He sidles up behind me, wrapping his arms around me and planting a kiss on my neck. He's just taken a shower and his hair is damp. I giggle like a teenage girl as he rubs it against my cheek. "Last night was incredible, baby," he says against my ear.

"Sure was," Mikey mumbles his agreement with a mouth full of cereal.

"It was." I agree as I turn in Liam's arms and kiss him softly.

"It's a shame we have to go upstate tonight," Mikey groans. "You're only back one day and we have to work."

"Tonight? You'll be gone all night?" I pout.

"Yes, tonight," Liam sighs as he takes a seat beside me.

"Shane thinks we don't know it's because he wants you all to himself," Mikey adds with a soft chuckle as he picks up his bowl and drains the milk from the bottom.

"What?" I blink at them. "I'm not sure Shane is that bothered by my coming back."

Mikey almost chokes on his milk as he starts laughing, and Liam places a hand on my shoulder. "You couldn't be any more wrong about that, baby."

I open my mouth to reply, but I'm distracted by Mikey as he looks up at the open doorway with his mouth hanging open. I spin around to see what, or who, he's looking at and I almost fall off my stool when I see Erin walking into the room, wearing the same clothes she had on yesterday evening. Bile burns the back of my throat and I force myself to swallow it down as a wave of nausea and jealousy washes over me. She spent the night. With Shane?

"Close your mouth, Michael," she says coolly as she walks to the refrigerator and opens it, taking out a bottle of mineral water. She holds it to her forehead briefly, before opening it and taking a long gulp, while the twins and I stare at her.

"What are you doing here, Erin?" Liam eventually asks the question we are all desperate to know the answer to.

She rolls her eyes, taking another gulp of water before she answers. "I stayed over."

"Where the hell did you sleep?" Mikey asks with a frown.

"In Shane's bed. Where else?" she says with a smug grin as her eyes flicker to me and she looks me up and down.

I force myself to smile back at her. "Well, I'm sure you had a comfortable sleep," I say, when I really want to vomit on the table in front of me. I knew that Shane wasn't my biggest fan, but this just seems unnecessarily cruel. To sleep with her on the same night that I came home. I choke down tears and have to look down at my bowl so she won't see me, because I feel like I'm about to cry and that is so damn ridiculous. Clearly, she is the woman that Shane wants. She is the kind of woman he belongs with.

"Well, I have a meeting to get to. Bye boys. And Jessie," she says before she wafts out of the room.

"Ice queen!" Mikey says with a shudder as soon as she's left the room.

Liam puts an arm around me and kisses me softly on the top of my head. "There's no way Shane would go back there, Jessie."

I blink away the tears and turn to him with a smile. "It's none of my business what, or who, Shane does," I say with a shrug.

"Don't say that, Red," Mikey narrows his eyes at me. "I don't know what's going on between you two, but you need to talk to him. Preferably, you could fuck some sense into him. Especially if he did screw Erin last night."

"Mikey!" Liam hisses.

"What?" he frowns.

"So, tell us about Arizona," Liam says, changing the subject.

"It was hot and sticky," I say with a smile.

"Pretty much just like you then," Mikey chuckles as he walks around the table and wraps his arms around my waist.

"I'm not sticky," I arch an eyebrow at him.

"You were last night, Red," he laughs.

"Well, so were you."

"Hmm. And I can't wait to get hot and sticky with you again as soon as we can," he growls in my ear. "But I need to take a shower. Be good while we're gone today, won't you?"

"Always," I whisper before he gives me a long, sweet kiss and walks out of the kitchen.

"Why Arizona?" Liam asks when there is just the two of us remaining.

"I wanted to try somewhere hot. And it was far away. As different to New York as I could think of," I reply with a shrug.

"Why did it need to be so different from New York?"

I look up into his deep brown eyes. "I didn't want to be reminded of you and your brothers. Or the time I spent here."

"Damn, Jessie!" he winces.

"Not because I didn't miss you, Liam. Because it hurt too much to think about you all."

"Why did you run so far, baby?" he reaches for me and brushes my hair from my face. "Conor almost lost his mind trying to find you."

"I thought you didn't want me here," I whisper.

"Jessie," he sighs as he takes my hands, pulling me from my stool until I'm standing between his strong thighs. "You're one of us. That means from now on, you don't get to run away when things get hard. Okay?"

"Okay," I nod.

"Good," he says as his hands slide over my hips and onto my ass. "Because this place wasn't the same without you. None of us are the same without you."

I press my face against his bare chest, inhaling his clean fresh scent. "I'm not the same without you either," I whisper.

CHAPTER 41

JESSIE

Walking into the kitchen later that afternoon, I almost want to turn around and walk back out when I see Shane standing there leaning against the breakfast bar with his back to me. But, I suppose I can't avoid him forever and something needs to happen to break this tension between us.

"Afternoon," I say as I walk to the counter and pour myself a coffee.

"Afternoon," he says gruffly as he eyes me over the rim of his coffee mug.

The air crackles with tension and energy and I take a deep breath. "So, how are you?" I ask and then I groan inwardly for asking such a ridiculous question.

He clearly doesn't appreciate it. "Really? Two fucking months and that's what we're talking about?" he frowns.

I roll my eyes, more at my own stupidity, but there is no need for his moodiness. "Okay. Something more meaningful then? So, you and Erin are back together, I see?" I ask with a flash of my eyebrows as the pang of jealousy gnaws at my center.

"Why did you come back here, Jessie?" he snaps, ignoring my question.

Jessie? I think I prefer him calling me Hacker. That was always our thing.

"Conor asked me to."

He shakes his head. "That's not a reason."

I stare at him, but I don't answer.

"So, why did you come back here?" he frowns.

"I just told you."

"That's what made you come back, not why."

"I don't understand what you want from me, Shane."

"How about the truth?" he snarls. "I appreciate it's not always your first instinct, but you should try it some time."

I slam my mug onto the counter and walk over to him. "I came back here because Conor asked me to. Because I missed him, and your brothers."

"Because you still love them?" he narrows his eyes at me as though he's trying to see inside my soul and it makes me feel too open and vulnerable around him.

"Yes!" I snap. I don't admit that I still love him too, because I can't bear to give him the satisfaction of knowing. He has made it perfectly clear how he feels about me.

His dark green eyes burn into mine and I fidget under the heat of his gaze. As much as I try not to, I can't help but picture him lifting me onto the kitchen island and fucking me senseless, and the images in my brain have the heat flushing over my chest and cheeks and between my thighs.

"That's the whole truth?" he growls.

"All of it," I lie and then I walk away before I make a complete fool of myself and beg him to take me to his bed and hate fuck me like he did the last time we were together.

LATER THAT NIGHT, I'm struggling to sleep. Despite the warmth of my room, I am cold. Conor is working at the club and the twins are out of town and my huge king-size bed seems empty without one of them in it. I get out of bed and make my way to the kitchen to make some chamomile tea, hoping it might warm me up. Passing the den, I notice Shane inside. He is sitting in the darkness, staring out of the window at the full moon. I should leave him in peace but something about seeing him sitting there all alone makes my heart ache for him.

I walk over to where he is and sit on the other end of the sofa. "Beautiful, isn't it?" I say, reminded of the night he took me to his spot on the lake and quite literally promised me the moon. And I promised him I would never leave him. I swallow the sob that catches in my throat at the thought of how I let him down so badly.

He sighs deeply, and I realize I've probably made a mistake sitting here with him. No doubt he was enjoying some time alone. But I'm here now so I may as well say my piece. "Look, Shane. You've made it perfectly clear how you feel about me. And I totally understand that. I know we're never going to be what we were…" I trail off because it hurts to say those words out loud.

He turns to me, the moonlight highlighting his handsome features and his muscular shoulders in the darkness. His eyes search mine, waiting for me to finish my sentence.

I take a deep breath. "But, can we at least try and fix whatever the hell is going on between us? Even if it's only so that we are able to sit in the same room together."

"Why? What would be the point, Jessie? We will never be what we were to each other."

I close my eyes as I remember all the memories he and I have made together in this place. How his touch sets my skin on fire. How he makes me step up time and time again and be a better version of myself. "Because nothing is right here when things aren't right between you and me. All I'm asking is for us to try to forgive each other, even if we can't forget. I made a mistake, Shane. A huge one, I know. But I'm only human. I know how much it cost you to let me in, and how much it must have hurt when I left." I brush a tear from my cheek as he sits there, unflinching. "If I could change it, I would. I hate myself for betraying you all like that." *Especially you.*

He doesn't answer me. Instead, he turns back to the window. I stand up and wipe away the tears that are running down my cheeks. At least I tried. I don't know what else I can say or do to prove to him that he can trust me.

I walk past the back of the sofa and as I pass him, I instinctively reach out my hand and run my fingers through his thick hair. It sends a raft of emotions whirling through my mind. I love his hair. I love running my fingers through it. I love everything about him. Perhaps I owe him the truth, even if he doesn't want to hear it. "I suppose if I'm asking you to give us a chance to be more than enemies, I should be completely honest and tell you that I didn't just come back here for your brothers. I missed you too," I whisper before leaning down and kissing the top of his head. I walk out of the room and head back to bed, hoping that one day he might be able to forgive me for leaving.

I LIE IN BED, staring at the ceiling and wondering what time Conor might be home, when my bedroom door opens. Immediately, I smell the distinctive cologne and my stomach somersaults. "Shane?" I whisper.

"Can I come in?" he asks.

"Of course," I sit up slightly as I see his silhouette approaching the bed. My breath sticks in my throat and I swallow. He lies down beside me and places his hand on my stomach. I'm wearing a t-shirt and I'm beneath the covers, but despite the layers between us, I still feel the heat from him searing my skin.

"I missed you too, Hacker," he says softly.

Hacker! I smile in the darkness. "You did?"

"Yes," he replies, his voice thick with emotion. "So fucking much." He reaches for my hand and lifts it to his lips, kissing my fingertips softly and making every nerve ending in my body come alive with energy. "But it doesn't change anything, Jessie," he says with a sigh as he lets go of my hand again.

The pain of his words almost chokes me and I stifle a sob. "Are you and Erin a thing again now?"

"No. I never slept with her."

"But, she said..." I draw in a breath as I recall the hurt I experienced when she walked into the kitchen with that huge smile on her face.

"She said what?" he frowns at me.

"That she spent the night in your bed."

"Well, she didn't lie. She did spend the night in my bed, but I wasn't with her. We had a few drinks to celebrate a deal she'd help me close. She could never handle her liquor. She was wasted, so I let her have my bed. I slept in my office."

"Did you undress her?"

"No. I took off her shoes and then I covered her with a blanket."

"Oh?" I whisper and then we lie here in silence, our breathing matching breath for breath and the air filled with tension and unspoken truths. I shift my position slightly and nudge his body and I swear I hear him groan softly.

"I wish things could be different, Jessie," he whispers. "I wish that I could be like my brothers and let you back in. I want nothing more than to kiss you right now and tell you that everything between us is okay. But I can't, because it's not and I'm not sure it ever can be. And I can't pretend that it is, because I can't kiss you and not fall in love with you all over again. It took so much faith for me to trust you. I don't have any left. I let down all of my walls with you..."

"I know," I say as tears roll down my cheeks and I don't bother to stop them. "You're breaking my heart, Shane, but I understand, and I'm so sorry that I destroyed your trust in me. I'm sorry I destroyed us."

"Hey," he brushes the tears from my cheeks. "It's not all on you, sweetheart. I promised we'd be just sex. I should have made sure it stayed that way."

"No, you shouldn't." I shake my head. "I'm glad we were so much more than that."

"But why? When it hurts so fucking much?"

"I know that it hurts now. But I would feel this every day for the rest of my life for one more moment like that with you. It was worth it, wasn't it?" I turn to look at him and can see the pain in his eyes even in the faint light of the room.

He brushes the hair back from my face. "Yeah," he smiles at me before leaning forward and pressing a soft, chaste kiss on my forehead. "Night, Hacker," he whispers before climbing off the bed and walking out of the room.

CHAPTER 42

SHANE

*a*s I walk down the hallway to the kitchen the following morning, the sound of her laughter drifts out into the hallway. I contemplate turning around and going back to bed, because as happy as I am for my brothers to have her back, it hurts too damn much to see her.

"Morning, bro," Conor walks up behind me and throws an arm around my neck. "You joining us for breakfast? Mikey's made pancakes."

I groan inwardly. But, fuck! This is my house and if Jessie is sticking around then I'd better get used to it, and quickly. Besides, I could use her help finding Alexei. "Yeah," I say, and we walk to the kitchen together.

"Did you and Jessie get a chance to talk?" he asks.

"Yeah. We spoke last night."

"Oh?" he frowns at me.

"What?"

"She was alone this morning when I got home is all."

"I said we talked Conor. We didn't fuck!"

His frown deepens and I roll my eyes. "We straightened things out. We're good. But we'll never be what we were," I tell him and admitting that out loud to him is like a knife slicing through my heart.

He shakes his head almost imperceptibly and continues walking.

I stop in my tracks. "What?" I snap.

"I didn't say anything," he holds his hands up in mock surrender.

"You don't have to speak for me to know exactly what you're thinking."

"Well, if you already know what I'm thinking, you already know that I think you're being a stubborn ass about this."

"You think I'm being too hard on her?" I scowl at him.

"No, Shane. I think you're being too hard on yourself," he says before he heads into the kitchen.

I walk into the room a few seconds after Conor, right on time to see him pulling her up from Liam's lap before lifting her onto the breakfast island and tongue fucking her mouth while she wraps her legs around him. Fuck! Me!

"Morning, bro," Liam shouts with a smile on his face that I haven't seen in weeks. Mikey tosses blueberries into his mouth while he waits for the pancakes to cook on the stove. I feel like I've walked into a fucked up porno version of Little House on the Prairie.

"Morning," I reply, and the sound of my voice makes her pull back from Conor. Her cheeks flush pink and she whispers something to him that makes him set her down on her feet.

"Morning, Shane," she says quietly as she walks back to the table and sits down again, on a chair this time.

"Jessie," I say with a nod as I take a seat myself. I look at my cell phone but my eyes keep being drawn to her thighs as she sits there in Liam's t-shirt and probably fuck all else. My cock hardens at the memory of her naked body and all of the things I did to it. And the thought of all the things I'd still like to do to it.

"What are your plans for today, Angel?" Conor asks as he kisses her head and sits down beside her.

"I was hoping to do some digging on Alexei."

Thank Christ! Something to distract me. "Do you have any leads yet?"

"Nothing concrete. But I've found some financial records today linked to the house in Connecticut where he took me. The funds have been funneled through at least four different companies, but I think I've found a common denominator that will identify some other properties Alexei might own. It will only take a little more digging and then I'll have a list of possible places where Alexei could be hiding, and then we can go from there," she says.

Fuck! I forgot how good she was. She got more in two days than I have in two months.

"Well, the sooner you get me those addresses, the better. Because we need to act fast. It won't be long before he finds out you're back here."

"About that," she says as she looks between me and Conor. "I can handle Alexei. I don't want any of you getting-"

"He came to our club and shot three of our men, Jessie," I say to her. "We are all in this together."

"Yeah, Red," Mikey says as he walks over and places a gigantic stack of pancakes in the center of the table. "There's no way we're letting you deal with him on your own."

"Besides," Liam adds as he sits on the other side of her and takes hold of her hand. "He stole you from us, and we owe him for that."

A flush creeps over her cheeks and she rewards him with a smile that makes me want to bend her over this table and fuck her brains out. I swallow as I try and maintain some level of self-control. Everything I said last night was true. I can never trust her again, so I can never go back there. But I guess my cock didn't get the memo. Asshole!

"We want Alexei almost as much as you do, Jessie," I say.

She smiles at me too and I have to look away before all of my blood rushes straight to my cock.

"Why not get the word out that I'm back, and then we can bring the fight here?" she offers as she helps herself to a pancake and places it on her plate.

"No!" Conor and I reply at the same time.

"Why not?"

"Because we're not using you as bait," Conor snaps.

"And because we'd prefer the element of surprise," I add. "If we sit back and wait for him to come to us, we lose that."

"Okay. It was just a thought," she shrugs.

"If you can find out which of those properties belong to him then we've got something to go on," I say as I take some of the remaining pancakes.

"Okay," she nods. "I'll get on it today. Any chance I could use your computer? It's got more juice than my laptop and it will probably take me the whole day?"

"Sure. After breakfast?" I offer.

"Great. Thank you," she whispers.

Jessie and Liam cleared the dishes after breakfast while Mikey, Conor and I discussed club business. She disappeared to her room about five minutes ago and I pray that it was to put on some clothes before she spends the day alone in my office with me.

I sit at my desk and sure enough, a few moments later, Jessie appears in the doorway wearing jeans and a hooded sweatshirt. The relief that I'm not going to have to stop myself from staring at her all day is equal to the disappointment that she has completely understood and respected what I told her last night. We have spent so many hours in this office together, during which she rarely wore any clothes. As a rule, she prefers to wander around this apartment in nothing but one of our t-shirts and a pair of panties. The fact that she is fully dressed today should make me happy, so why does it piss me off so much?

"You ready now?" she asks softly as she pulls her hair up into a pony tail.

"Yeah. Come on in."

It's early evening by the time Jessie and I stop working. She has had her head bent over the computer for seven hours, only stopping for a quick sandwich when Mikey insisted she eat something. I've made calls and chased leads and generally been impressed by how quickly and efficiently she works. It has been a relief that we've both been so busy because it has stopped me thinking about all of the times I've fucked her in this room.

Conor walks through the door, making Jessie look up from the screen. "How are you two getting on?" he asks as he flops down onto the sofa.

"Good," she says with a smile.

"Our hacker did good," I say and I don't miss the look of pride on her face. "Jessie found the name of the company that owns Alexei's house in Connecticut, as well as another property in the area. I've sent some of our men to do some recon on the other property and they haven't reported back yet. But I suspect we might have found Alexei."

"Fuck! You two work fast," Conor says with a grin.

"It was all Jessie. I've been looking into this fucker for two months and had nothing."

"You helped," she says.

"Yeah, as your gofer!"

She opens her mouth as though to reply and I wink at her, making her smile and blush.

"So, what's our next move?" Conor asks.

"We need to strike soon, before he finds out Jessie is here."

"How soon?" she asks.

"Like tomorrow night soon? Are you both okay with that?"

"Yes. The sooner he takes his last breath on this earth, the better as far as I'm concerned," Jessie replies.

"Fine by me," Conor adds with a nod before he stands up. "You done for the day?" he asks her.

"Yep." She switches off the computer and stands too. "You didn't need me to do anything else, did you?" She turns to me.

"Nope. We're all done," I say and wince at my choice of words, because me and her really are all done.

"Good. I need you to help me shower before I go to work." Conor winks at her and then he slides his hand on to her ass as she reaches him, and squeezes before leaning down and kissing her. She stands on her tiptoes and kisses him back before the two of them say goodnight to me and walk out the door.

CHAPTER 43

SHANE

*I*t's after midnight when I finally head to bed. Conor and the twins are working in the club and Jessie must be in bed because I didn't see her when I passed the den. As I near her room, I stop outside for a few seconds. How easy it would be to walk in there and crawl into bed next to her, running my hands over her soft, warm skin and tasting every inch of her before I bury my cock in her sweet cunt. I groan out loud. Why the hell did I go and fuck everything up? Just sex. That was what we were supposed to be. And if I had kept it that way, I wouldn't have been so fucking cut up about her leaving. We could have gone back to just sex.

But there is no just sex with Jessie. She is under my skin, and my heart sinks as I realize she probably always will be. I want to hate her but I just can't. I love her but I don't trust her. And I don't know how I'm going to be able to live under the same roof as her and deal with these feelings, because it damn near killed me to see her walking out of my office with Conor earlier today, knowing they were probably on their way to fuck and being acutely aware of the fact that she and I will never get to do that again.

"No! Volk!" the high pitched shriek comes from Jessie's room and I don't even think before I burst into the room and run to the bed. I heave a sigh of relief that she's just having a nightmare, having half expected to come face to face with the elusive Wolf from the terror in her voice.

I turn on the lamp on her nightstand and sit on the bed beside her as she whimpers and thrashes beneath the covers.

"Jessie," I say softly and she shouts something unintelligible, but the terror on her face is real as beads of perspiration run down her forehead.

I place my hand on her arm and note the heat from her skin. "Jessie!" I say, louder this time, and her eyes snap open.

"Shane!" she gasps as her eyes dart around the room.

"Yeah, it's just me. You were having a nightmare."

She swallows hard and wipes her forehead with her hand. "He was here," she stammers.

"The Wolf?"

She nods furiously.

"There's no-one here but you and me, sweetheart. Promise," I say as I brush her damp hair from her forehead.

A single tear runs down her cheek and it breaks my heart to see her crying.

"Jessie," I breathe, desperate to touch her.

"Are you sure there's no-one here?" she looks up at me through her long, dark lashes.

"One hundred percent. I've been watching the security monitors all night. You're safe."

"Well, except from you," she laughs softly and I smile at her. "You're the most dangerous of them all, Shane Ryan." She reaches up and brushes her fingertips over my cheek.

I swallow hard as I use every ounce of restraint not to pin her down and fuck her until I forget why I shouldn't.

"Will you stay with me for a little while? Just until I fall back asleep?" she breathes and I wonder if she's purposely trying to make me hard or whether my body is just hardwired to react to hers this way.

"I don't think that's a good idea."

"Just to lay here with me. I promise I won't try to take advantage of you." She smiles faintly but I see right through her because she is trembling in fear. Whatever the Wolf did to her has left scars that I suspect will never heal.

"Well, now you're just taking all the fun out of it," I say as I lie on the bed beside her. I resist the urge to wrap my arms around her because I know where that will lead. She will rest her head on my chest and I will smell her hair and feel the warmth and the softness of her body against mine, and then I will be completely fucking undone.

She shifts onto her side until we lie face to face. "I enjoyed working with you today," she whispers. "You are a very good underling."

"Well, don't get used to it, Hacker. I give the orders around here, remember?"

"How could I forget?" She smiles and the tension starts to slip from her body and her eyelids flutter. "Thank you for staying with me."

"Any time. Now get some sleep."

"Yes, Sir," she purrs and the sound makes a direct line to my cock. I bite my lip as I watch her eyes closing and she drifts back off to sleep. I could leave now because I've done what she asked of me. So, why am I still lying here staring at her.

CHAPTER 44

CONOR

*M*usic thumps in my ears as I make my way through the crowded club toward my office at the back. A blonde wearing the tiniest yellow dress I have ever seen pushes her tits up against me as I squeeze past. I shake my head at her and walk on by. She's not my type, but perhaps twelve months ago, I might have taken her to my office for a quick fuck. However, I have no interest in any woman other than Jessie, who I hope is being fucked by my older brother right now, because I need the two of them to work their shit out.

I've missed her these past two days. It was nice having her all to myself for a while, but I love the way she is with my brothers. She makes all of us happier and easier to be around. She makes our home a much better place, adding something that none of us even realized was missing. I realize I've got a goofy grin on my face from thinking about her, when one of my bouncers approaches me and asks me what I'm so happy about.

"What?" I shake my head and remember that I'm supposed to be a tough guy down here.

"I said what are you so happy about?" Chester asks.

"Nothing that you need to concern yourself with. What's up?"

Chester signals that we should go into my office and we walk the few yards to it and step inside, where we can hear each other better.

"So?" I frown.

"We got some girl out front demanding to get in here to see you, is all."

"You recognize her?"

"No. But she's tall. Brunette. Your usual type," he says with a shrug. "At least, she used to be."

My frown turns to a scowl now. "Why didn't you just let her in anyway?" I ask. I don't know who she is and I don't particularly want to see her, but if she's my previous usual type, then she would have no problem getting into this club.

Chester looks down at his feet for a split second before he answers me. "Well, here's the thing. We couldn't let her in 'cause she's got a kid with her."

"A kid?"

"In a stroller," he nods.

I have no idea what's going on and I don't like being blindsided like this. "Did she give a name?" I ask him.

"No, Boss," he shakes his head. "She just said that you'd recognize her, and…" He doesn't finish his sentence, instead he just looks at me with a strange expression on his face.

"And what, Chester? For fuck's sake! Stop talking in riddles."

"She kinda nodded her head to the kid, you know? Like you'd recognize him?"

"What the fuck?" I snarl, wracking my brains to think of any woman I've slept with in the past few years who I could have knocked up. But I can't. I always use protection, at least until Jessie. But Chester is right. Brunettes used to be my type, and while I didn't ever take many up to the apartment in recent years, I certainly indulged in my fair share of brief encounters in my office. But I was always super careful. I always used a condom. And I always disposed of it myself. "How old was he? The kid?"

"I dunno. A baby still. Maybe one?"

"Fuck, Chester! This is all I need."

"She's probably just trying it on, Boss. After some greenback to make her disappear quietly. I told her to take a hike, but she's starting to make a scene."

"Take her around the back and tell her I'll meet her there," I say with a sigh.

"Want me to come with her?"

"No. I'll handle it myself," I snap.

Chester nods and walks out of my office and I pour myself a whiskey and knock it back, enjoying the liquid warming my throat on its way down. Whoever the hell this woman is, I'm convinced that it's not my kid she has with her.

A FEW MINUTES LATER, I step into the alleyway behind the club, pulling the collar of my jacket up against my neck in the icy wind. The mystery woman is standing waiting for me, complete with kid in a stroller. It's after midnight and there isn't much light back here, so I have to strain my eyes to see her. Chester was right. She has long dark hair, big tits and a pretty face and is exactly the kind of woman I used to fuck around with, but I have never seen this one before in my life. And I have never been wasted enough to fuck someone I wouldn't remember. So who the hell is she and what the hell does she want with me?

CHAPTER 45

MIKEY

*A*s I look around the packed club, I strain my eyes to spot Liam and Conor, but I can't see either of them. The last time I saw my twin he was throwing a few underage college kids out, while trying to fight off a particular handsy one who seemed to have taken quite a shine to him. He asked me to help him out but I was too busy laughing at the panic stricken look on his face.

Six months ago, being felt up by a twenty year old with hardly any clothes on would have been a good night out for him, and me. But that was before Jessie! Two more hours in this place for me and then I'll be joining her.

Liam and me have been pulling double shifts almost every night in this place while Conor was away, so tonight is my turn for an early finish. And that means I get Jessie all to myself. I cannot wait to crawl into bed beside her and fuck her senseless. My cock throbs at the thought of being inside her hot, wet pussy and the sound of my name on her lips when she comes.

I rearrange my cock in my suit pants to relieve the growing pressure and one of the barmaids notices me and gives me a huge smile. Damn. The pussy in this place is fine, and it's wall to wall every single night. But I have no interest in any of these women any more and that is as much is a surprise to me as anyone. I have never been in love. I used to think it was a crock of shit. But fuck me, I would die for that feisty little red-head upstairs.

I scan around for Liam and Conor again as I feel a hand on my shoulder. I spin around and come face to face with a guy about my age with a bright green Mohawk.

I frown at him.

"You're Mikey, right?" he shouts over the music.

"Depends who's asking."

"Jessie," he replies and the hairs on the back of my neck stand on end.

"Jessie?" I snarl at him, because as far as I know she is safely tucked up in bed about eight floors above us.

"She's looking for you. She asked me to find you for her."

I grab him by his shirt collar and he flinches. "What?" I push my face closer to his.

"A girl called Jessie asked me to tell you that she needs to speak to you. She's downstairs in the VIP area."

"What did she look like?" I hiss.

"I don't know. Hot. Red hair," he stammers and I release my grip on him.

"Was she alone?"

He straightens his shirt. "Yeah, man. She looked like she'd been crying."

"Fuck!" I push past him and make my way to the VIP bar as my pulse starts to race. What the hell is Jessie doing down here and why is she crying?

It's only as I push my way through the crowds of people that I think about the woman waiting upstairs in bed for me, who no longer has red hair because she dyed it brown when she was in Arizona. So, what the fuck is going on? I look around for my brothers again and grab one of our bouncers as he passes. "You seen Liam or Conor?" I ask.

"Conor went out the back a few minutes ago. Last time I saw Liam he was throwing those two kids out."

"Anything weird happened here tonight?" I frown at him.

"Nothing weirder than usual, Boss. Why?"

"Find my brothers and tell them to meet me in the VIP bar."

CHAPTER 46

JESSIE

*D*espite promising myself I would stay awake so I could spend some time talking with Shane, I must have drifted off to sleep because the sound of the door bursting open wakes me. My eyes snap open and my heart starts to hammer against my ribcage. Shane is still here with me and he jolts awake too.

"Shane!" Mikey shouts as he runs into the room. "They came to the club. The Russians. They've taken him."

Shane and I both sit up at the same time. "What? Taken who, Mikey?" he shouts.

It seems like my heart stops beating now as I look at Mikey's face, and then I see Conor running into the room behind him. I feel anger vibrating through Shane's body as bile surges up from my stomach and I fight the urge to be sick.

"Liam!"

Find out what happens next for Jessie and The Ryan Brothers in Ryan Retribution

ALSO BY SADIE KINCAID

If you'd like to find out what happens next for Jessie and The Ryan Brothers, you can preorder the next books in the series on Amazon now:

Ryan Retribution

Ryan Reign

He is the King of L.A, and she is his queen. Alejandro and Alana Montoya are hotter than hell in Sadie's L.A Ruthless series. Available on Amazon and FREE in Kindle Unlimited.

Fierce King

Fierce Queen

Do you love an age gap romance full of tension and steam? Find out what happens when the King of LA's daughter falls for his best friend in LA Ruthless Book 3.

Fierce Betrayal

If you'd like to read about London's hottest couple. Gabriel and Samantha, then check out Sadie's London Ruthless series on Amazon. FREE in Kindle Unlimited.

Dark Angel

Fallen Angel

Dark/ Fallen Angel Duet

ABOUT THE AUTHOR

Sadie Kincaid is a steamy romance author who loves to read and write about hot alpha males and strong, feisty females.

Sadie loves to connect with readers so why not get in touch via social media?

Join Sadie's reader group for the latest news, book recommendations and plenty of fun. Sadie's ladies and Sizzling Alphas

Printed in Great Britain
by Amazon